To AL

From NaNa & Pappy

Gnome Mountain

Nick Shears

DEDICATION

This book is dedicated to my family and to the Berkeley Springs outdoorsmen who shared their knowledge of the West Virginia mountains, a perfect setting to let gnomes run free.

CONTENTS

CHAPTER 1

Ty stood astride his bike on the ridge top. Wind rustled through the pines and he shivered in his sweat-soaked shirt. Grandpa's cabin was far down the mountain, shrouded in morning mist.

He'd seen nobody as he hiked up. A few weekenders' cabins lay deep in the woods, closed tight. The dust plume from Dad's old van had long since settled from his return to the interstate. There was no sign or sound of anybody for miles around.

Abandoned in the woods, I might as well have some fun, he thought.

He studied the bike beneath him. Chipped paint, stout frame, fat knobby tires. Could a bike found on trash day in the city be fit for the mountains? It was time to find out.

Ty dug in his heels and pointed the bike straight downhill. He lifted his feet to the pedals, released the brakes, and rushed ahead. Potholes and rocks jarred him violently. The woods seesawed back and forth.

Brake levers full back against the handlebars, he still accelerated.

The first turn was on him in seconds, a switchback left. Leaning hard uphill, he skittered over loose gravel and dirt, wobbled, jabbed a foot in the dirt uphill, and cleared the turn. Next came an even sharper turn right and Ty tensed in terror. The bike slid sideways to the road's edge and then, sickeningly, lurched sharply over the top and went airborne.

The frame and rear wheel fell away as Ty clutched desperately to the handlebars. Next came a violent bounce and he was thrown free and headlong into woods and dry, hard dirt.

A sapling snapped and skittered across his helmet and forehead, opening an ugly gash. The bike bounded off, landing first on the front wheel, then on the back, before coming to a crashing stop, its wheels spinning frantically in the air.

Soon all was quiet except the wind in the trees and Ty groaning and catching his breath.

From up the mountain came a skittering sound. A small figure ran from one tree to the next, stopping to peer nervously at the fallen boy.

Finally he stood casting a shadow over Ty, wrung his hands, and began muttering excitedly. "Oh my, oh my a biggie's come crashin' knocked himself on the noggin," he said. "No problem making contact. Emergency clause applies."

"All right then," the little man said, as Ty stared in amazement.

"Me name's Marvin," he said brightly. "I'm a gnome, most likely the first one you've ever seen. Good guess?"

Ty nodded, eyes wide, taking in the sight of a short, dark-haired man with a pointy red hat, bushy eyebrows, a green jacket with wood toggles, large strong hands, furry knuckles, leather shorts, and huge muscular calves.

"Rules say we can make contact with biggies in emergencies. Even so, I'll have a lot of paperwork to do. But on with it, on with it, you've got a nasty gash, good bit of bleeding. But I'll fix you up right proper."

Ty tapped his forehead gingerly and could feel blood in his blond hair.

"Just got a few things to pull together to make an ointment. Probably in a bit of shock you are. Back in a moment," he shouted, producing a bone-handled knife.

Marvin scampered off, running from tree to tree, scraping and stirring brownish pine goo on a smooth piece of bark. "Oh what a busy gnome am I, fixing this biggie in the wink of an eye," he sang.

Next he hopped three times on a tree stump, dropped to his knees at Ty's side, and lathered a gooey, pungent paste on Ty's forehead.

"Good grief, what's that?" Ty asked, recoiling at the smell. "Some kind of spell and magic potion?"

Marvin sighed. "I'm afraid not. No magic, just pine sap. The singing and jumping around are just theatrics. The sap works wonders, though. Ever try to get pine sap off? It locks onto a wound and heals it up good as new. Bleeding's stopped already. Growing up, my gnomies and I were as daft as you, but healed up right as rain."

Marvin paused and looked around. "So was that your dad who gave you the lift?"

"How'd you know that?" Ty asked, startled.

"I heard from a friend. You can meet him." Marvin

pulled a carved wooden pipe from his back pocket, put it to his lips, and produced a deafening bird call. "Basic crow call for warning of a hawk," Marvin explained. "You hear it all the time."

In moments, a large red-tailed hawk sliced in from the sky and landed in the tree overhead.

Marvin pointed to the ground at his side and the bird dropped directly to that spot. The magnificent bird turned its head to eye Ty intently.

Marvin pulled a leather pouch from his waistband and produced three long pieces of smoked deer jerky. He held one out to the bird, took one for himself, and handed the third to Ty.

"We call him Spike," Marvin said. "We don't know what his hawk friends call him."

Spike gulped down his jerky then looked eagerly at Ty, who quickly tore his piece in half, ate one bit and tossed the other to the bird.

"Spike," Marvin asked, "who is the boy you saw arriving here today?" Spike lifted a feathered leg and pointed his talons at Ty.

"Where did he drop you?" Marvin asked, then had a sudden inspiration. "Spike," he said excitedly, "fly down and circle the house where this boy went."

Soundlessly, Spike lunged forward, spread his wings, skimmed over treetops, banked sharply and twice circled an old log cabin, far from the road.

Marvin leapt to his feet. "That's it," he said, "that's Travis' old cabin. You must be wild Travis' grandson!"

"You knew Grandpa Travis?" Ty asked, amazed.

"Sure we did. He was a fantastic friend of the gnomes. No biggie ever had the run of Lonesome

Mountain's gnome cave like he did."

"That clinches it," Marvin added. "Some time you've got to come meet my gnomies back at the cavern. They'll be thrilled to meet Travis' grandson. But right now, I think you better go back to the cabin and rest."

Marvin looked Ty over carefully. "Are you okay to walk? I'll come with you and see you home."

"Yeah I'm okay," Ty said, struggling to his feet and retrieving his bike. "Let's go."

Together they walked down the bumpy road beneath tall white oaks and maples. Through the driveway's knee-high grass they trudged, approaching the cabin with its wooden porch and walls of vast notched, stacked logs.

"This cabin says a lot about old Travis," said Marvin. "Few biggies could even get their arms around these logs. But Travis wrestled those vast logs into place all by himself with just ropes, pulleys, and his bare hands."

Ty pushed open the door and saw that everything was exactly as it was when his dad dropped him off. To the left of the door on a worn old couch was a suitcase, duffel bag, bags of groceries, and a carton with a woodsman's supplies – a compass, maps, mouse traps, folding saw, first aid kit, matches, freeze-dried food, a space blanket, a field guide to the Appalachian mountains, and other necessities. To the right was an old wood-burning, cast-iron stove.

Not entirely primitive, the cabin had electricity to run lights, an electric hot plate, the cistern pump, and the water heater. The walls were neatly finished with pine planking with a warm, honey-colored varnish.

"Home sweet home," Marvin said, hopping up on the sofa. "You'll be fine here, Ty. But tell me, why did your dad drop you off by yourself?"

"It's unsafe back home. My Dad and I live in a little apartment over a bar called Chesapeake Tavern. There are lots of fights and arrests."

"Oh yes," Marvin said, eagerly jumping to his feet and thrashing his arms about. "Travis owned that bar. There were many insults, fights, pranks, and jokes. It sounded like great fun."

"Well maybe it was fun back then but it's too dangerous now. Last night my friends Bucky, Billy, and I were walking back to the apartment after playing basketball. Suddenly one guy came running out of the bar with another guy after him. The second guy smashed the neck off a beer bottle and hurled the rest at the other guy. The bottle whistled right by our heads. One of us could have been hurt or killed."

"That's not good," Marvin said, shaking his head earnestly.

"No, not at all," Ty agreed. "Anyway, the cops came and Officer Pete, who's a friend of ours, made dad promise he'd get me out of town for the summer at least, far away from the drunks and other 'undesirables.'"

Ty shook his head. "This morning I woke up to find dad up early, had the van packed, and was cooking a huge breakfast. By noon he'd dropped me with this gear, assured me I'd love it here and drove off."

"Of course, it doesn't help me get used to things when straight away I meet a guy who says he's a gnome and that there are more like him up in the hills. Mind you I am grateful you patched me up. But seriously, are you just – I don't know what the proper word is – a vertically challenged man?"

Marvin laughed. "Can a man big or small do this?" As Ty watched from inside, Marvin dashed out, paused for a moment between two trees, leapt left then right, bounding from one tree to the other until he reached the treetops. Then, he sailed to a tall sapling, grabbed its top, bent it down to the ground and slid off, landing neatly on his feet.

Ty was stunned. "Wow, that's amazing. Still, I've had a bump on the head. I'm pretty sure this is just a crazy dream. I'm going to lie down on that bed and have a nice nap. I expect it'll just be me here when I wake up."

Marvin laughed. "If so, that won't be true for long. My boys are restless and ready for a night out. At dusk you'll see a few of us show up to check on you and take you to town for some adventure, if you're ready."

"One more thing," Marvin said earnestly. "I hate to have to say this because I know you come from good people. But don't be tempted to call a TV station saying you've got a story to tell about gnomes. First, think about how that would sound. Second, realize we've been down this road. We've helped put people in the looney bin who've tried to capture us or take our pictures. You understand that?"

"Sure," said Ty. "Whatever you are, you're the best and only friend I've got at the moment."

"You could do worse," Marvin said. "We gnomes are loyal, if a bit crazy. See you this evening."

As Marvin turned and walked up the mountain, Ty

went inside to lie down. He fell asleep immediately and slept until five.

He woke hungry, having eaten nothing since breakfast in Baltimore. He went to the stove, emptied a large can of Dinty Moore beef stew into a pot.

Soon the stew was hissing and popping over the heat, sounding and smelling as it did when Ty and his parents camped together when he was little.

Ty poured the stew into a bowl, carried it out on the porch, sat in grandpa's worn rocker, and watched the sun glint off the meandering river below. I'm sure grandpa spent a lot of time sitting right here like I am, he thought, comforted at the thought.

Ty sat finishing his dinner for a few minutes. Then, as he stood to go back into the cabin, he heard a distant rustling in the leaves. Squirrel probably, he thought, and went inside and closed the door. A few minutes later he heard a gentle padding sound and soft breathing from the front steps.

He peered through the grimy window panes and saw a thin, stray-looking black Labrador with his nose to the door, head down and looking haggard.

"Oh my God," Ty yelled, throwing open the door. "Midnight is that you?" The dog thumped his tail, walked into the cabin, and flopped down on his old canvas pad by the fireplace. Next, he rolled over on his back and pawed at the air, asking to be patted.

Ty obliged and hugged the dog. "Midnight," he said. "We looked for you after grandpa died. We thought you'd tried to get help but nobody had seen you. It's been three months. You've been living in the woods alone. You look half-starved, you poor thing."

Ty found and opened the single can of dog food in the kitchen and scooped it into a bowl.

"While, you're eating I'll pour you a warm bath. You're filthy and stink but we'll get you squared away. Man, it's great to have you back. Dad will be relieved, too. I'll have to call and let him know next chance I get."

Ty had Midnight clean, dry, and sound asleep when he heard a knock at the door. He leapt to his feet and rushed to meet his visitors outside to avoid waking Midnight.

There he found Marvin and two other waist-high gnomes solemnly twiddling pointed hats in their hands. Oddly, one had a carved, life-sized wooden gnome under his arm.

"Ty, these are my buddies, Nate and Jasper. Jasper's carrying his look-alike we call J2. He comes in handy when adventuring around biggies."

As they shook hands, Marvin asked, "Why'd you rush to the door so Ty? Have you got a pretty, blushing little wood nymph in there you're entertaining?"

"If so, I gnomie Nate myself for the job instead," cackled Nate, taking a deep bow toward the door, and doffing his hat to reveal his long curly red locks.

"No," Ty said with a laugh. "The only one in there is Grandpa Travis' dog Midnight. He's sleeping. He was exhausted, dirty and half-starved but he's already doing much better after a bath and something to eat. I do need to find a place I can buy him some dog food, though."

"We were planning to go adventuring in town

anyway," Marvin said, "so we can get dog food or whatever you like."

"That would be great," Ty said. "I'll leave the screen door unlocked so Midnight can nose his way in and out if he needs to. But I bet he'll sleep straight through the night, as worn out as he looks."

"Jasper," said Nate, "you're in charge of transport. What do you have lined up for us this evening?"

"The usual, the poker express, courtesy of Thurston."

"What's the poker express?" Ty asked.

"Thurston lives on the next road upriver. We have his yard miked, though it's hardly necessary, the way he and his wife Shelley get to hollering. Poker's always the cause of the argument and we root for Thurston. That's because when he goes to play poker, we sneak along for the ride. We know he's going tonight because we've already heard them carrying on about it."

"Anyhow, he's got a big blue tarp in the bed of the truck. We climb in under that and we're off."

Jasper went on quietly. "We gnomes run close to the ground and, though it's humiliating, we can always freeze and pose as garden gnomes if spotted. You, on the other hand, will need to scurry on all fours now and then if you're going to hang with us. You'll be too tall otherwise."

Ty wondered what he was getting into. "Okay, I guess."

By this time, the unlikely group was arrayed high to low behind a tree in Thurston's driveway. When he runs for the truck, we do, too, but from the blind side.

Got it? Here he comes now.

"Thurston you'll be going to poker tonight over my dead body," Shelly yelled.

"Well good thing my truck's got plenty of clearance," Thurston hollered back.

The screen door flew open and Thurston came running at a full sprint. The gnomes dashed ahead, vaulted the tailgate and dove quickly under the tarp, with Ty scrambling in behind.

Ty and the gnomes curled up, biting their fists to stifle their laughter. "Oh my," Ty said, "we've got to help Thurston patch things up or we'll be walking the six miles to town next time."

Marvin agreed. "Definitely. We depend on biggies a lot. They help us out and we help them out, anonymously, of course. You'll see how it works."

It was near dark as Thurston pulled to a stop in front of a green wood-frame house on the outskirts of Little Falls. Peeking from under the tarp, the stowaways could see Thurston greeted at the door and ushered to a round table in the front of the house.

Thurston sat facing the street with a view of his truck through a tall sash window. With his back to the window sat a player in camo overalls and a John Deere cap. Two other players rounded out the foursome.

Ty and the gnomes waited for Thurston to look away, then quickly leapt from the truck bed and huddled between the front window and a large bush.

"Listen," Marvin said, "Shelly's main problem with Thurston's gambling is that he loses more than he wins. She'll be waiting up for Thurston, mad as a cloud of hornets. But if he wins some decent money for a change she might forgive him."

The player opposite Thurston is Big Mike, Marvin explained. He's the one who usually wins.

"We'll wait a few minutes until it's completely dark then get in position below the two windows. Ty and I will watch for a round when the other two players have folded, there's a lot of money on the table, and we're just down to Thurston and Big Mike.

"Jasper, you stay in front with J2. I'll watch through this bush here and when I give a thumbs up, you peek over the sill, write down Big Mike's cards and hold the sign up to the window," Marvin said, handing Jasper a piece of cardboard and a marker.

Marvin looked around to make sure nobody was watching. "Thurston will catch on. We want to stick with it until he wins at least one big pot. Got it?" Jasper nodded.

Darkness closed in, reassuring Ty and the gnomes that they wouldn't be spotted from the street. After ten minutes, Marvin gave the thumbs up to Jasper, who quickly popped up, scribbled the number 10 three times on the cardboard and held it up for Thurston to see.

Thurston's eyes went wide but he regained his composure before the other players noticed. He also threw another $20 bill onto the table. Big Mike matched the bet. Thurston then threw in another $20. Big Mike's eyes narrowed but he threw in a $20, too.

As all four players leaned in to see the cards, Big Mike caught Thurston shooting one last glance at the window. Big Mike looked down at Thurston's cards, saw he'd lost the hand, then leapt to his feet and raced to the window, eyes blazing.

"There's a tiny man in a tall hat out there," he yelled. "What the hell's going on?"

"Decoy with J2 then hide behind the garage!" Marvin said sharply. Jasper quickly laid J2 on his side and the four raced down the driveway.

Big Mike made it outside first. "Who put this freakin' garden gnome in my yard? Is this a prank? Did it fall out of someone's truck?"

Big Mike eyed Thurston suspiciously. "What were you looking at out that window Thurston?" he asked.

"I just looked up when I saw some headlights on the road," Thurston said innocently. "It was a truck with a nice set of ladder racks, the kind I need to keep from scratching up my cab. I've been meaning to get some like that."

"Speaking of which," Thurston said, "I've got to get up early to finish replacing those rotted-out fascia boards on the Miller's cabin and re-hang their gutters. They've got some renters coming in tomorrow evening."

"Well alright," said Big Mike, grudgingly. "I guess it's been your turn to finally win a night's poker. We've been cleaning you out for quite a few weeks now."

"Even a blind squirrel finds a nut now and then," Thurston said, shrugging. "See you next time."

Thurston walked out with the other men, said goodbye, then got in his truck and drove back down the road toward home.

Marvin nodded toward the main road. "Now part

two of the plan. Let's try to hop a ride to the big city, get some dog food for Midnight and see what other mischief we can get up to."

"The big city?" Ty asked. "I assume you just mean Warm Springs, right, not Hagerstown."

"That's right," Marvin said.

The group waited until Big Mike and his pals went back inside, then Marvin scampered out to the road and picked up a carton run over by a truck. He tore off a flap, wrote "FREE" on it, and leaned it up in front of J2.

"You know the drill from hitching the ride with Thurston," Marvin said. "We lie low in the weeds over here until somebody stops and picks up J2. Once they've got J2 stashed in the bed, we jump aboard. Of course we need it to be someone going up over Lonesome Mountain toward town. If we see somebody stopping going the other way, Ty you run over, pick up J2 and tell the folks you saw it first."

Just as planned, when the fourth truck passed, they saw brake lights glow red, the driver fetched J2, and climbed back in cab. Just as the door slammed, the four scrambled aboard and hunkered down in the open bed out of sight.

"Oh man, look at the stars," Ty said "With the light pollution in the city you never see a night like this. And the full moon's so bright, I can actually see my shadow."

After a pause, Ty pointed to the road behind. "And look over there. A possum's crossing the road, slow as can be."

The gnomes laughed. "You might just make it as a

country boy," Nate said.

The truck crested the ridge and began the long run of switchbacks down the mountain and into the rustic resort town of Warm Springs.

"I didn't get a good look at our driver," Marvin said. "But from what I saw of the truck and his build, I'm pretty sure we've ridden with this guy before. He lives behind the football stadium at Warm Springs High School. We hop out there, hide J2, and jog a hundred yards across and you know where we'll be?"

"Finger Lickin' BBQ!" the gnomes said in unison. "Hush puppies, ribs, brisket, beans, collards, cornbread," moaned Nate. "We'll have sweet tea, pie, maybe a cold beer."

"Nate, you're just 82, you're too young to drink," he said, shooting Ty a glance.

"What?" said Ty, shocked. "I thought you were kids like me, younger maybe."

The gnomes laughed. "That's a common misperception," Marvin said, "or common rather among the few biggies who know about us in the first place. But, yes, gnomes can live to 200. And we keep our strength, wit, and dazzling good looks. It balances out the nuisance of living in hiding."

"Well what if you just came out into plain sight?" Ty asked. "What would happen?"

"It'd be horrible," Nate said. "We wouldn't be free to roam. People would search their land for gnomes living underground and kick us off. They might ship us to reservations like the Indians. They'd make us pay taxes, start school at 6 instead of 42. We'd get arrested for jumping boxcars. They might not even let us drive, thinking it's unsafe for one gnome to work the pedals, while another steers."

As Marvin predicted, the truck turned right off Valley Road and parked behind the high school. Fortunately, the driveway was dark and the driver saw nothing more than a few fleeting shapes disappearing across the field."

After a moment's pause, the man yelled in anger. "Hey, bring back my gnome. You can't just steal a man's gnome like that, you thieving punks."

"We are from the gnome liberation front," Marvin yelled from the darkness. "Gnomes can't be owned any more than people can. Read about it online"

Ty turned to Marvin as they strode across the dewy field in the dark. "Is that really true?"

"Absolutely," said Marvin. "Gnome liberation started among biggies actually. French activists saw there were thousands of garden gnomes in ones and twos in fenced off gardens. The understood these gnomes yearned to be free. They gathered gnomes from around the country and set them free together, deep in their ancestral woods."

"Here in the U.S. you can't imagine how exciting it was when that Travelocity website started showing gnomes coming out of their petrified state and being driven around the country in convertibles. So now we've got a mixture of live gnomes and gnome figures. It is a bit confusing."

Marvin finished this explanation just they reached the parking lot behind the "Finger Lickin' Good BBQ" restaurant.

The restaurant was in a low-slung building that

looked like a small café from the outside. But from the inside one saw it had expanded down the block, buying and knocking out walls into an old home and a warehouse.

The newest room had windows at street level that cranked open for ventilation. Portions were huge and customers often left their plates half full of barbecue and sides.

"Ty," said Marvin. "There's a family in there now almost ready to leave. The kids are looking restless and they've just handed cash to the waitress. Hurry in and ask if you can sit in that front room. Then take this sack, scrape the leftover food into it, and hand it out the window."

Ty walked in and smiled at the hostess. "I'm by myself and would like some space where I could lay out my newspaper to read. Could I sit in the front, where there's plenty of room?"

The hostess obliged, and soon Ty had handed the leftovers out to the waiting gnomes. As Ty ate his own dinner, the gnomes ate theirs, having run around back and climbed into a broken-down old step van nestled in some brush.

"Next stop is Food Lion," Marvin said, referring to Warm Springs' only grocery store. "We'll meet you there. We'll sneak through the woods rather than risk being seen on the road."

"I tell you what," Marvin added, "here's a twenty. Go into the Goodwill next door and buy three kids' Halloween costumes off the rack in the back, then leave the bag by the dumpster behind the store. We'll see you inside."

Nate and Jasper rubbed their hands together, eagerly.

"Okay," Ty said. He pulled out his phone. "Meanwhile I better call my dad while I have a cell signal. Don't worry, the word 'gnome' won't cross my lips."

"I'm so glad you called," said Ty's dad, Walt. "I was worried about how you're doing there all by yourself."

"I really haven't felt alone at all. One great help is that Midnight came back. I was sitting alone in the cabin this afternoon when he just came snuffling up to the door like he'd never been away. He was dirty, hungry and very tired but he's almost back to his old self after I fed him a good meal, washed him, and pointed him to his pad for a good long nap."

"That's wonderful," Walt said. "He's such a great dog, and after all the time we spent looking for him, I was afraid we'd never see him again. I've got another great bit of news, too. I've lined up a job for you with a guy named Thurston, just one road over."

Walt explained that Thurston was a handyman who had helped Grandpa Travis. Walt had called Thurston to see whether he needed a helper and learned that Thurston could use help starting the next morning, repairing storm damage.

"If that goes well, you could work for him as much as you like," Walt said. "And I know you'll do a great job. You've always been handy and able to pitch right in fixing things in the bar and at Grandpa's cabin."

Walt added that Thurston had said he was going grocery shopping in Warm Springs that evening but that Ty should just swing by his house in the morning about 7 a.m.

"Funny you should say Thurston, Dad," Ty said. "I'm outside the grocery store now and I just saw him pull into the parking lot. I know it's him, because I see his name painted on the truck. It says 'Thurston Martin, Handyman.'"

"How'd you get to town?"

"Oh, I hitched a ride," Ty said. "And if I'm going to work for Thurston, chances are good I can hitch a ride back with him. I'll go ask him in the store. Also Dad, one thing I wanted to ask. Do you remember the way Grandpa used to laugh when we asked him if he ever got lonely? He'd say he had plenty of company but never said who it was."

"Yeah, I remember that. I didn't know what to make of it. He was very smug like he had a secret nobody would ever guess."

Ty said goodbye to Walt and glanced over at the woods behind the shopping center. He saw the gnomes watching him closely. Better hurry, Ty thought to himself. He walked quickly into the Goodwill Store and picked out a bear costume, a lion costume, and a red devil costume, all in kids' sizes. He then paid at the counter and left the bag out back as instructed.

Next, Ty jogged into the store, scanning for Thurston. He wanted to introduce himself and ask for a ride home.

He spotted Thurston over by the flower counter at the front of the store. He was wearing a blue WVU cap, a white pocket t-shirt, and brown Carhartt work pants.

Thurston looked a bit over 50, had a weatherbeaten face, brooding brown eyes and a muscular build. He stood uncertainly studying a bouquet of roses.

"Thurston Martin?" Ty called out.

"Yes," said Thurston, turning.

"Hi sir," said Ty stretching out a hand and introducing himself. "I was just on the phone with my dad as I was walking up. He told me you were looking for a helper for your handyman business. I'd love to do that, sir. I'm pretty handy already. And I'd be happy to learn whatever else I need to know."

"That's great," Thurston said, turning back to the flowers. "I'm afraid what I need help with right now is picking up something to help smooth things over with my wife. She's pretty sore at me but with buying some flowers and having won good money at poker tonight, I think the trouble will blow over."

"Well, to play it safe you might just want to get a box of chocolates, too. My dad used to buy them for my mom when she was mad, though, she left home eventually anyway. How is it you know my dad?"

"Oh, he was visiting when I installed a well pump for your Grandpa Travis some years back," Thurston said.

Ty nodded and furtively glanced over Thurston's shoulder, an angle that gave him a good view across all six checkout lines.

Suddenly, out popped the brown bear with a large, round watermelon. He bowed, set it on the ground, stepped onto it with one foot, then the other, causing it to roll crazily in circles with the bear aboard.

"Billy," the bear yelled in a high voice, "let's do our

trick quick before mommy comes back from the potty."

Out popped the lion while the bear did backflips, along the front of the store, including two directly from one conveyor to another, sending cashiers and customers shrieking in all directions.

For the finale, the devil appeared as the bear heaved the melon high in the air. The devil did a handspring into a bicycle kick that sent the melon soaring toward the ceiling.

"Yay, yay," yelled the costumed creatures in husky voices and caught the melon just inches from the floor."

Customers and staff looked on in amazement. Some clapped, some scowled at the recklessness, and others looked for the creatures' mother.

The three gnomes, still in their costumes, bowed and dashed out the back of the store, circled around front, and dove under the tarp in Thurston's truck.

Shortly afterward, Thurston and Ty came out of the store, climbed in the truck and drove back over Lonesome Mountain. Ty fell asleep in the front seat and woke only as Thurston pulled into Grandpa Travis' driveway.

"Thanks Thurston," Ty said. "I'll be over at your place at 7:30. Do you mind if I bring Travis' dog Midnight along? I'm sure he'll enjoy the company. He won't run off, chase anything, or go in the house."

"Sure," Thurston said, backing out of the driveway, this short conversation having given the gnomes time to scramble off into the shadows until Thurston left.

"You could have hired out with us," Marvin said,

sounding a bit hurt. "Still can. We'll stop by tomorrow night, take you on a tour of our cavern. We run some businesses there. You'll be surprised."

"Oh but we don't have what Mr. Baker has," Jasper said. "He has such a beautiful daughter, makes me dizzy just to think. I wish I could make gnomie courtship polka dance with her. Probably just a nuzzle in her blonde hair, though, and I'd fall down hypnotized."

Midnight had heard the truck and came out through the pet door, to greet Ty, who fed him a fresh can of dog food, changed and climbed in bed. He turned out the light and, before falling asleep, felt Midnight hop onto the bed and curl up at his feet.

CHAPTER 2

Ty woke early the next morning to the sound of a woodpecker drumming. After breakfast, he and Midnight took a shortcut over to Thurston's, walking an old logging road through the woods. The sun had just crested the mountain and burned holes in the fog, allowing sunlight to mirror off the river.

As Ty walked up the driveway, Thurston came down the front steps carrying a travel mug and looking Ty up and down.

"Alright Ty, in those work clothes you look the part."

Midnight jumped in the back and they drove a mile upriver to the Bakers' cabin and announced their arrival with the sound of gravel crunching under the tires.

Tim Baker walked out to meet them, a smile on his face and hand outstretched. He wore jeans, sneakers, and a sweatshirt. Ty judged the man to be about his father's age, in his late 40s.

Thurston introduced Ty. "You two have something in common," Thurston said, "both from Baltimore."

"Whereabouts?" asked Tim.

"East of Patterson Park"

"Isn't that a rather rough area?"

"Yeah, well that's the reason I'm suddenly out here for the summer, to stay safe. Just walking down the street, I nearly got brained as a bystander to a fight."

"Yikes," Tim said, then turned to Thurston. "So, as I told you on the phone, a tree blew down in last week's storm. It hit right where the gutters attach to the fascia boards, knocking the gutter clear off. Plus there are a lot of limbs and branches down. Follow me, I'll show you."

They walked around back where they saw a screened porch and heard guitar playing stop abruptly. Ty saw a freckled blonde girl his age wearing jeans and a t-shirt.

"Ty, this is my daughter Casey," Tim said pointing through the screen. "Casey, you remember Thurston. This is his new helper, Ty." They all waved and said hello.

Thurston and Ty worked through the morning. At one point, Casey came out to bring them lemonade.

Thurston noticed Ty watching Casey return to the house. "Don't think about it," Thurston said. "She's got a rich boyfriend, who drives around here weekends in his own BMW."

"You don't think she wants to trade up to a handyman's apprentice?"

Thurston laughed. "Only advantage you'd have is that Tim doesn't like the boyfriend much, thinks he could be trouble."

Thurston and Ty worked until midafternoon. After they'd packed up the truck, Ty stood by while Tim settled the bill.

As Thurston walked to the truck, Ty turned back.

"Mister Baker, I just moved here and don't know anybody my age. Would you mind if I asked Casey to go for a walk with me by the river? That is, if she'll say yes."

Tim smiled. "Not to worry son, I'll insist on it. Casey's had nobody her age to hang out with this weekend. It will do her good to get some fresh air."

"Thank you sir." Ty turned to face the house and noticed Casey quickly step away from the window. She was curious at least. Ty walked to the door and knocked.

"Casey, would you like to come for a walk with me down by the river?" he asked haltingly. "I've been here just a couple days now. I've made some friends but they're in their eighties. I'd love to hang out with someone my age."

Casey hesitated. "I'd have to ask my dad."

"He's okay with it. He told me so."

Casey rolled her eyes. "So you're plotting with him? What a schemer you are."

Ty felt his face flush. "It's not like that. I asked his permission."

"You're quite proper, mister handyman. But what if I say no?"

Ty smiled. "I'm afraid you're stuck with me. Your dad said he'd insist you go."

Casey's eyes narrowed. "Good grief. Two can play that game. Sure, let's go."

She turned and started walking briskly down the driveway. Ty called Midnight and ran to catch up.

"Check this out," Casey said leaning toward him and

whispering in his ear. "Watch me mess with both of you at once."

She turned to wave to her dad, then suddenly slapped Ty hard on the rump, cackling at Ty's and her father's stunned expressions.

"You've got moxie young lady. I'll give you that."

"And you've got a good vocabulary mister tradesman's apprentice. Meanwhile be sure you know that was for shock value. Don't get your hopes up."

"I see who really has his hopes up," Ty said, pointing ahead at Midnight, who was trotting a few steps ahead with a heavy stick in his mouth.

A few minutes later, they reached the river and stopped in the shade of a huge sycamore tree. Midnight dropped his stick at their feet, stared at them intently and woofed.

"You'll have a friend for life if you throw that stick into the river for him," Ty said.

Casey nodded and picked up the stick. Midnight ducked his head and shoulders, thumped his tail, and shivered in anticipation. Casey threw the stick with a smooth motion, sending it sailing out over the river, with Midnight wheeling in pursuit.

"Wow, I'm falling for you," Ty said. "What an arm you have."

"Softball shortstop. You better be fast getting to first base or I'll throw you out."

Ty burst out laughing. "Excuse me?"

"Oh jeez." Casey blushed and shook her head.

"Freudian slip?"

"Don't flatter yourself, Romeo. Anyway, I told you I've got a boyfriend, Vincent."

"And don't you flatter yourself. I've already flirted with every girl I've seen today. You just happen to be the only one."

"Touché."

Ty and Casey walked in silence a bit, then started talking about their schools in Baltimore. Casey went to a school in the wealthy suburbs. Ty went to a gritty, inner-city school.

"What do you and your friends talk about?" Ty asked. "The usual gossip, clothes and stuff?"

"Thanks for the vote of confidence. No, truth is a lot of my friends don't talk about much else and it does get a bit old. How about you?"

"Well, I go around from one clique to another, the jocks, the hipsters, the brainiacs, the misfits, etc. I feel like I fit in everywhere and nowhere."

He paused. "Now I've a got this new challenge, trying to adjust to living alone on this mountain all summer."

Ty told Casey about his grandpa, father, the tavern, and how he'd been dropped off alone on Lonesome Mountain.

"I'm afraid I'll just be looping through my thoughts and having nobody to share them with. This morning I had two voices arguing in my head. One said "The unexamined life isn't worth living." The other said, "The examined life isn't worth the lost sleep. What do you think?"

Casey laughed. "You know Ty, you're quite the woodsman philosopher. I'll grant you, you're fun to talk to. Meanwhile, could you show me your grandpa's cabin? I'd like to see your hermit lair."

"Sure." Ty pointed to a gap in the trees. "There's a shortcut that will take us there, an old trail."

As they walked, Casey asked, "You mentioned something peculiar earlier. You said you'd made some friends in their eighties? Who was that?"

Ty immediately regretted having let that slip. But then, as if on cue, he was stunned to see Jasper leap from behind a tree with Nate and Marvin desperately trying to pull him back. It was too late.

"A wood nymph," cried Jasper. "A biggie goddess. Oh I am smitten. Cupid has struck me with his mightiest arrow. At your service, lovely maiden. Take me home to your princess castle."

Casey looked wide eyed at the gnomes, then at Ty. "Ty, are these dwarves?" she whispered under her breath. "I mean vertically challenged, whatever? And this jabbering one is crazy. Are the others like this?"

"I'm new to this, too," Ty said, watching in amusement as Marvin and Nate hustled Jasper up the hill, scolding him as they went. "Total breach of protocol, Jasper, we'll be in huge trouble with Gnome One. You hopeless love-struck gnome. You stay here and be quiet. Jasper plopped down cross-legged but waved enthusiastically at Casey.

As Marvin and Nate approached, Ty quickly explained how and when he'd met the gnomes.

"I've known about these guys for just a day," Ty said. "They've invited me to visit their cavern tonight."

Ty turned to face uphill where Marvin and Nate stood. "It's good to see you again. This is my new friend Casey." The two gnomes nodded, trotted down, and eagerly shook hands with Casey. Jasper leapt to his feet again, afraid of being forgotten, and waved madly.

"Gnomes," Ty said, "you had offered to take me to your grand cavern. Could Casey come along, too? I know it's earlier than we agreed. But I doubt her parents would like her out late in the evening."

Nate and Jasper nodded their heads eagerly. Marvin thought for a moment. "Gnome One may be mad at us briefly, but he is so very fond of girls that he will quickly forgive us."

Ty tapped Casey on the shoulder so she tipped her head over his way. "Are you okay with going along?"

"I can't believe this is even happening, but I wouldn't miss it for the world."

"I'm so glad. If I weren't with another 'biggie' as they call us, I might be afraid I was going crazy."

"We do have some procedures we're going to need you to follow," Marvin said. "We must walk in silence from now on. And, when we're within a few hundred yards of the cavern, we'll have to blindfold you before leading you into the cavern. After the entrance is closed you can take them off again."

After hiking uphill for about half an hour, Marvin ducked onto a narrow path and began winding his way to a rocky ledge jutting out over their heads from the steeply wooded mountainside.

Here Marvin stopped and asked Ty and Casey to bend down so he could affix their blindfolds. The peculiar group began walking again, sometimes all joining hands so the three gnomes could pull the two biggies sharply uphill. Midnight scampered happily along behind.

Blindfolded, the biggies walked on the level for a few minutes then down a few steps, stopped and heard panting and the grinding of stone on stone. Next they were led to a space sheltered from the blowing of the wind and rustling of the trees.

Marvin removed the biggies' blindfolds and faced a steep rocky trail leading deep within the mountain. The footing was uneven – sometimes boulders, sometimes steps cut in the stone. Overhead were great wooden timbers like inverted wishbones supporting the rock above. A small but rapid stream ran beside the trail and set wooden water wheels spinning, turning the shafts of old bicycle headlight generators. These generators powered dim but steady light to guide their way.

After a long descent deep into the mountain, the group came to a heavy oak door. Marvin knocked and shortly a tiny sliding window flew open, revealing a darting, curious eye.

"Greetings!" thundered a voice within.

"Oh very honored guests are you," said Marvin happily to the biggies as the heavy door slowly creaked open. "A big celebration is afoot, I wager."

"I am Gnome One," said the barrel-chested man before them. He had bright eyes, a red knob-like nose, a wide handlebar mustache, and a thick, long bushy beard. He wore the traditional red, pointy hat and long tunic with a leather belt cinched around his belly.

He grinned, exposing gleaming teeth and winked at Casey. "Ah Casey, you are even lovelier in person than you are on our gnomecams, which we have hidden on the road and the path approaching our modest underworld village."

Gnome pointed to three gnomes with badges on their chests. "And what do the security gnomes do when you appear on their gnome screens? They exclaim their love for you, they weep and dream about you ... until their wives beat them back to their senses."

"Oh hush you windy old fool," yelled one stocky gnome woman pushing her way through the crowd of gnomes still spellbound by Casey. "I'll teach them some respect."

"That goes for you, too, you crusty old toad," cried another woman, who slapped her husband's lovesick face.

"Stop it now," Gnome One thundered. "Don't spoil our celebration honoring our guests. There will be plenty of time for scolding and pining later."

He stared down the last combatants. "But before we start the tour and party, please bring the signing book."

A gnome hustled to the front bearing a worn leather bound ledger. "Here it is your oneness."

"Ty," called Gnome one. "Come read us the last inscription."

Ty stepped forward and took the book from Gnome One's hand. "It says Travis Franklin, October 1, 1992. That's my granddad! To think he was right here."

At this utterance, the gnomes erupted in cheers. "Hooray for Travis, great friend of the gnomes."

"Travis, one of the great ungnomes," cheered Gnome One. "A great ambassador to gnome man's land."

Gnome One turned to Ty. "To be elected Gnome One you have to enjoy puns. We do have our little quirks, we gnomes." He waved toward the back of the cavern. "Come along you two. Let's give you a quick tour. Then we'll go back and get the party started."

Torches lined the walls and their flickering threw moving shadows against the rough rock walls.

Close to the entrance was a large workshop where workers were making and painting garden gnomes of wood and poured plaster. "We sell these on eBay to raise biggie money," Gnome One said.

Deeper in the cavern were small caves full of bunk beds.

"You sleep wherever you like. We wear the same clothes so you just throw yours in the laundry kettle and grab a new set off the drying racks. Men wear red hats, green tunics, brown pants, and boots. Women wear red hats, colorful blouses, skirts and pointy clogs for women. Families stick close when the kids are young. Later the kids are such a handful that we mostly give up on discipline and herd them off where they can carry on as much as they like. Here's a kids' room now."

Gnome one opened a heavy door to reveal a sight shocking to Casey and Ty. Little boy and girl gnomes, some no taller than quart milk cartons dashed about madly with the strength and dexterity of adults.

The springy little gnomes ran at great speed across the floor and right up the walls until their feet were skyward and their cone hats pointed down at the floor. Even as they fell, they'd race their legs upside down for effect, spinning upright just before impact.

As they watched, two girl gnomes began shoving each other. "Thunderpants," shouted one. "Knobby knees," cried the other. The first then lifted the other off her feet by her pigtails.

Suddenly the children spied Casey and Ty and pointed. The others stopped, too, and a hush fell over the young gnomes.

"Visitors from the biggie kingdom," gasped a freckled young gnome, pushing aside his stout, straw like bangs for a better view.

Picking up on the kingdom theme, Ty grabbed two toy crowns from a toy chest and put one on his head and one on Casey's.

"Who likes fairy tales?" Ty cried out, drawing a huge cheer. "And who wants to see a biggie princess kiss the prince and make him the happiest biggie prince in the whole world?" Another huge cheer went up.

Casey turned and wagged a finger at him. "You are such a naughty scoundrel," Casey said.

Ty pointed to his cheek. "Just put it right there, fair maiden. Don't disappoint the kids, or me for that matter." As the gnomes cheered, Casey gave Ty a quick kiss on the cheek.

"It's almost time for their music hour," Gnome One said. "Would you like to sing them a song?"

"Do you have a guitar handy?" Ty asked.

"Most indefinitely. We gnomes love live music and dancing up a racket with our knobbed boots on."

Grown gnomes came gathering around to see what had silenced the kids. A gnome handed Ty a guitar, causing the little gnomes to cheer and clap.

"I'd like to play a song that was one of Granddad Travis' favorites," Ty said, *Chantilly Lace* by the Big Bopper.

Ty and Casey were amazed that the little gnomes belted out:

"Chantilly lace and a pretty face, and a pony tail hanging down, a wiggle in the walk and giggle in the talk, makes the world go round..."

The little gnomies loved the song but Ty noticed several grown gnomies looking anxious as the song ended.

Moments later, several of the little gnomies yelled "wrestle" and the whole lot of them joined in a vast tussle.

Gnome One sighed and tipped his head toward the door. "When this happens we just close the door and leave them be. They can't play outside as much as they'd like, so we let them have a jolly good wrestle several times a day. After that they'll enjoy reading and children's hour in the exercise room. I'll show you that next."

Gnome One looked over his shoulder at the group of grown gnomes, who were also getting restless. Ty and Casey looked back in time to see one gnome pants another. The victim pulled up his britches and grabbed an egg from a basket carried by a passing gnome. Without a word, he lifted his assailant's cap, smashed the egg on his head and neatly replaced the hat before the egg could seep out over his oversized ears.

"Don't mind being an egghead," the other gnome said, amiably. "Makes my hair a bit more manageable.

My nose hairs are the most devilish. For instance, when I bend this one and let it go, it sounds like a banjo."

Ty and Casey exchanged an amazed and appalled look. "I think it's pretty clear gnomes are a different species, not just little humans," Ty said. Casey shuddered and nodded.

"Here we are at the gym," Gnome One announced, pointing into a large cave. Inside was a suspended rope course, ladders, slides, and heavy boulders.

The grown gnomes dashed in and soon were careening about much like the children. They climbed, swung from ropes, threw boulders back and forth, wrestled, laughed, and exchanged mostly good-natured insults.

"How many gnomes are there?" Casey asked. "And how do you remain undiscovered?"

"We have eighty five here now," Gnome One said. "Some gnomes come here from other gnome lands. Some leave to become 'air gnomes' or 'topsiders.' Air gnomes refuse to live underground. That means they have to live in the most remote areas where few humans go."

Gnome One lowered his voice. "Marvin still pines for an old childhood friend of his. Her family moved to Wyoming to become air gnomes."

"As for how we stay undiscovered, it's become both harder and easier," Gnome One added. "Satellite imagery has gotten better and better, so any vegetables we grow have to be in very small patches, for instance. At the same time, people have become what we call 'screen heads.' They get fatter, don't get out in the outdoors as much as they used to, and even if they do get out in the woods, they're walking with their heads down searching for a phone signal rather than gnomes."

"How about a guy like Travis?" Casey asked. "How did he find you?"

"It's the observant old woodsmen like Travis who do catch on to us," Gnome One said. "What caught his eye were fresh, small footprints he'd see in pine woods. Thing was, it was outside deer season. Only thing you can hunt legally then is squirrel. But Travis knew squirrel hunters don't hunt there because squirrels that feed in pine woods taste like turpentine. How many people these days are going to know that? With that he knew there were active trails by little people."

"How did he find out for sure that there were gnomes?" Casey asked.

Gnome One shook his head and chuckled. "Travis told us folklore had it that gnomes liked moonshine liquor. Travis had a very small still of his own. No reason for it really, other than that it had been handed down to him. He set the still out in front of his cabin. Next morning he saw footprints. So over the next week he made a little batch and set a couple small tin cups of moonshine out. Sure enough it was gone by morning."

Ty burst out laughing. "That's Travis for you," he said. "I can just picture him, pleased as can be, spying out through a knot hole in the cabin door."

"Yes, indeed," Gnome One said. "First night he stayed up to watch, he caught one of our gnomes, who told him everything. Security had a fit. Of course, a few of them promptly went down to Travis' and started drinking, too."

Gnome One dropped his voice to a whisper. "I might have stopped down there a time or two, myself. But the best thing about old Travis was his inventions. Did you ever hear about the Tyvek fliers?"

"Tyvek, you mean the house wrap you attach to sheathing before hanging siding?" Ty asked.

"That's the stuff. Tyvek is light and rip proof and there was lots you could dumpster dive during the last building boom. He made little hang gliders good for us gnomies."

Most of the roads run straight up the mountain, Gnome One explained. This meant you could point your hang glider straight downhill and fly it down to the river, maybe circle above the trees a few times if the wind was right. Afterwards, two gnomes could carry one back up on foot.

"He built one big hang glider for himself," Gnome one added. "We've still got it, stashed away. You could try it some time. It's really not dangerous. You're just a few feet off the ground but still flying because of the grade. You or Casey want to try it?"

Ty cast Casey a look. She was trying to teach juggling to some little gnomies. She had overheard the conversation but shook her head.

"Maybe another time," she said. "Meanwhile, I'm afraid I need to be getting home or my parents will worry about me."

The biggies said their goodbyes and promised to return another time. "Gnomies, stop by in the evenings," Ty said in parting. "I should be home by 5 p.m. during the week."

Marvin placed the hoods over Casey and Ty's heads and led them to the road, from which they walked back to Casey's cabin.

"Wow, this has been the craziest day of my life," Casey said, as they arrived at her front door.

"Mine, too," Ty said. "When are you driving back to Baltimore? Tomorrow morning?"

"Yes, I'm afraid so."

Ty looked away, trying to hide his disappointment. "When are you coming back?"

"Two weeks from now," she said. "Vincent's coming, too."

"Hey, I may be home next weekend to see my dad. Could we get something to eat maybe?"

Casey chuckled and shook her head. "Boy, you're persistent aren't you?"

"What can I say? I've had a great time with you today. You're great fun and easy to talk to."

Ty produced a pencil stub and scrap of paper. "Here's my phone number," he said, writing. "I won't ask for yours so you don't feel pressured. With the bad cell service, if you do call, you'll probably have to leave a message unless I'm in town, on the road, or back in Baltimore."

Casey looked at Ty's outstretched hand holding the paper. Slowly she reached for it and put it in her jeans pocket. "I'm not promising anything," she said.

"Fair enough," Ty said. "Have a safe trip home."

Ty and Casey stood awkwardly, for a few moments. "Goodnight Ty," Casey said, then walked inside.

CHAPTER 3

Tuesday afternoon Gnome One gathered Marvin and the other elders around the stone table near the cavern entrance. "Gentlemen, we must post the latest garden gnome orders. And with Ty living in the cabin, I think we'd better forego borrowing Travis' ATV without permission."

"Gnomie you old sod," Nate protested. "Twas my turn to give the thunder beast a great throttle twist and terrify all creation."

"Stop your grousing, Nate we're back on the bikes until Ty gives us leave to use the ATV."

"Gnome One," Marvin pleaded. "At least, spare me riding the wee pink girl's bike with the streamers. I'm 82 and deserve to ride in dignity."

Gnome One sighed. "Very well, I'll squire that one myself. Load the crates so we can be off at sundown."

With Gnome One in the lead, the intrepid bike brigade was off. "To market to market to sell our fat gnomes, then leap on our steeds to carry us home," sang a jolly voice in the back.

The gnomes pedaled the river road for two miles without incident. But hearing an oncoming truck, they swerved to take cover, landing knee deep in a drainage ditch, the truck's headlights sweeping the bank just over their crouched bodies.

The soggy bunch crossed the river at the low-water bridge and proceeded toward town.

"Oh misery," muttered Nate shifting his bottom as he rode. "Bog water right through me knickers. Chafing now. Itching to come. Pestilence."

Soon the bedraggled convoy rode into town then turned east for three blocks down a dark lane, rather than venture onto the main road. They stopped at the second-to-last house before the river bank. There they ducked into a yard with a rusty metal mailbox marked "Gallagher."

The neighboring houses showed more signs of life. The house to the left had a large tractor-tire planter and a carport sheltering a V8 truck engine. The one to the right had several wooden deer cutouts as decoration, plus one chubby garden gnome, which the live gnomes each greeted quietly to avoid attention.

"Yo," muttered one, with a fist bump. "Sup gnomie," hissed another. "Fair tidings my stalwart friend," said Gnome One, shaking his head. "Gnomies, please, you hail from the wood, not the hood."

The procession rode their bikes into the back yard and hid them in the dew-soaked grass. From within the house glowed a single bulb hanging from a lamp cord in the small kitchen. The gnomes climbed the steps and knocked lightly at the door.

An elderly woman in a faded green house coat walked to the back door and opened it.

"Ah it's you gnome gentlemen," she said, standing aside to let them in. "Everyone tells me you gnomes don't exist, that I've gone soft in the head, rattling on about gnomes. But you look real to me, as always."

"So we are, Ms. Gallagher," said Gnome One. "Real or not we've brought you some nice fresh-cooked meals. I'll just pop them in the fridge for you."

"Thank you, boys," she said. "When the family visits, they say I'm looking fit and plump, no need to put me in a home, not that they could afford it anyway."

"What do we ask in return?" Gnome One asked.

"Just the truth, that I help shy craftsmen mail their gnome statues to eBay customers."

Gnome One clapped his hands in delight. "Marvelous, Mrs. Gallagher, that's perfect. Thank you. We'll drop our packages in the post, collect any checks of ours from your mailbox, then be on our way home."

"Oh now don't be in such a hurry. I don't get much company." She paused, noticing Nate squirming.

"Why's that little man tugging at his britches so unhappily? Oh he's all wet. All you young fellas, take off those wet pants and let me throw them in the dryer for a few minutes. Then have a cup of coffee. I've just made a fresh pot."

Soon the gnomes were sitting around the kitchen table in their drawers, legs dangling in the air, sipping fresh coffee, and smacking their lips.

"Ah Mrs. Gallagher," said Nate. "You're a fine woman. You'll be a great catch for your next husband.

You're a sight for sore eyes you are."

"You'd be a fine catch yourself, though you are a bit odd looking, a bit like a gnome even."

"Not at all, Mrs. Gallagher," Gnome One said in alarm. "You're quite mistaken. Heaven forbid."

After finishing their coffee, pulling on their dry clothes, and exchanging more pleasantries, the gnomes excused themselves and peered up and down the lane to ensure the coast was clear. Gnome One stood watch and waved them across the road to the post office, one by one, so each could put his boxes in the parcel drop.

Jasper was about to start his dash across the road when Big Mike suddenly opened his front door and stepped off his porch to walk to his truck. Catching sight of the gnome, Big Mike fixed Jasper with a fierce, suspicious stare and began walking toward him to investigate. Jasper froze.

As Big Mike approached, so did a large dog, the latter trotting up to Jasper from the dark lane. Mike stopped as the dog began sniffing around Jasper's legs. To Jasper's horror, the dog raised his leg and relieved himself copiously on Jasper's shoe.

Big Mike laughed and watched closely to see whether Jasper would move. Surely, he thought, nothing alive could withstand that without flinching. Finally Big Mike walked to his truck, climbed in, and drove away, mumbling to himself. "Ain't no live gnomes anyway, why did I even think that for a minute."

As soon as Big Mike was out of sight, the other gnomes laughed until they ached at poor, soggy

Jasper but then, sympathetically, stopped at Mrs. Gallagher's again to borrow a bar of soap, plastic bag, and a pair of her husband's old sneakers.

Jasper washed up with the garden hose, stowed his soiled shoe, donned Mr. Gallagher's oversized pair and the gnomes started their ride back to the cavern.

"Bye dearie," said Nate. "Don't go breaking the young town boys' hearts now, Mrs. Gallagher."

"Don't think I didn't used to," Mrs. Gallagher said. "More than one heartsick suitor came down this very lane howling at the moon over me."

"No doubt a line down the block, I'd wager," Nate said as they pedaled away.

Gnome One shook his head as he pedaled. "No need to wind up the poor old dear."

"It's all in good fun, gnomie. She's happy to natter a bit."

Soon the gnomes were beyond the town's last street lamp and drew level with Jimmy's Garage, where headlights threw white cones across the road.

"I bet that's young Daryl," said Gnome One, excitedly. "He's the one with narcolepsy. Falls asleep anywhere. Goes out like a light in the time it takes him to shimmy under a car on a creeper."

"Look at him now," added Nate. "Truck running, lights on and forehead flat against the steering wheel. Gnomes we must do our good turn and drive him home safely, all the better that he lives out our way."

Jasper clapped his hands in glee. "I claim wheel," he crowed.

"Pedals are mine," Nate added quickly, as the others groaned.

Gnome One looked troubled. "Nate, you'd better well remember which pedal is which this time. Have a heart for those who have to look out the window and see each near disaster."

Gnome One walked quietly to the passenger side, placed his hands on the fender, and stared expectantly at the other gnomes. "C'mon someone lend a hand already."

Jasper dashed to help, joining his hands with laced fingers to make a stirrup for Gnome One, who heaved himself over the fender, kicked one leg through the open window, then rolled neatly onto the passenger seat.

Gnome One righted himself and stuck his head out the window. "So fond of this old truck with its nice vinyl bench seat. The trick's just to gently slide young Daryl to the passenger side. I'll tug on the side of his belt from this side, you shove from the other."

Daryl stirred and mumbled something unintelligible but then settled back to sleep, tipping a bit sideways and snuggling his head peacefully into Gnome One's vast, springy beard.

The other gnomes sighed in relief, loaded their bikes in the cargo bed, then climbed in through the driver's window. Nate quickly got in driving position, settling on the floorboard and pulling his knees up to his chest, so his feet hovered just above the accelerator and brake pedal.

Jasper took the wheel and reached for the shifter handle on the steering column. "Oh I love this. I'm in 'P' for park. Should I select 'N' for nice or 'D' for dangerous?"

"None of this tomfoolery," Gnome One said firmly. "It's not too late for you two knaves to be left to ride your bikes home."

"No, no, we'll do your bidding," Jasper said. "Not to worry. A little bit of 'go' please Nate, if you would."

Soon the truck was crunching its way across the gravel lot and out onto the paved road.

"A little bit more go" said Jasper mildly. After a moment's pause he shrieked, "Full bore Nate like the devil's on our tail."

Nate stomped on the gas in surprise. Squirrels by the roadside raced up trees. Even a lumbering possum fixed the truck with its stare then wobbled away as Jasper cranked the wheel back and forth for a few terrifying moments. "Easy does it now," Jasper said.

Gnome One stared fixedly at Daryl, whose head lolled side to side but remained asleep. "Both of you out of the truck right now," hissed livid Gnome One. "Leave your bikes, socks and shoes. I want you to have some time to regret your recklessness."

"Gnome One," said Jasper, "I'd otherwise be happy to walk but just this morning I applied a lovely coat of cocoa butter to my feet, so tired from my gnomish chores. I'd hate to undo the therapy. Could I please keep my shoes and socks?"

"By coincidence, forsooth I did the same," said Nate.

"Alright, just get out of my sight," said Gnome One, exasperated.

That excitement concluded, Gnome One and the remaining gnomes, drove Daryl to his house and pulled his truck quietly into the driveway.

Marvin asked the others whether they'd mind if he walked over to Ty's cabin for a quick visit. Gnome One and the others shrugged. "None whatsoever," said Gnome One. "Tell him we send a cheery hi ho."

The gnomes unloaded the bikes. Save for Marvin, the other gnomes wheeled their bikes up the mountain to the cavern, aided by the light of the moon and stars.

Marvin picked his way across the mountain for about half a mile, rather than walk down to the road and back up. He walked past hunters' tree stands and abandoned, rundown cabins. Finally Ty's cabin came into view, with a cheery glow from the lights inside and a curl of smoke from the woodstove coming from the chimney, a modest summer fire, just enough to cook over.

Midnight woofed inside so Ty let him out. The dog raced up to Marvin, threw his paws into Marvin's chest and bowled him over.

Marvin bounded to his feet, grabbed Midnight by the snout. "Try to catch me now you hell hound."

Marvin let go and raced to a small stand of maple saplings. He bounded back and forth between two trees, pushing with his feet and grabbing with his hands. Midnight barked and chased wildly between the trees as Marvin climbed to top of a tree, then clung to it as it bent double and groaned in protest.

Finally, Marvin let go his hold, dropped neatly to the forest floor then dashed twice around the cabin, Midnight again in hot pursuit.

"Expertly done," called Ty, who'd come out onto the porch to watch after hearing the commotion. "C'mon in. I've just cooked some chili and baked a pan of cornbread. Meanwhile, you're spoiling that dog. How am I supposed to give him a game of chase like that?"

"Ah, it's just practice. Sorry to be intruding when you're about to eat supper. It does smell mighty good, though." Marvin walked to the foot of the porch steps.

"Happy for the company," Ty said, extending his hand. Marvin offered his, which Ty grasped tightly and pulled, lifting Marvin into the air and depositing him neatly on the top step.

"What do you think I am, some sort of play thing?" Marvin huffed.

"Sorry, impulse thing," Ty said. "I'm still a bit incredulous on the gnome front. Lifting you confirms my eyes aren't playing tricks on me."

"Just my luck, I make my first biggie friend and he's a dimwit."

"So no chili and cornbread for you?"

"I'm not saying that, not at all."

The two sat down at table, and Marvin immediately began shoveling food in his mouth. "Oh you'll be a right good catch for a lady – a fine cook and likely thought passably handsome by girls, at least in dim light."

Ty rolled his eyes. "This from a stumpy, rude little troll, elf or whatever you are."

"I've a mind to box your ears, you numbskull, teach you some manners. Elves, trolls, and the like are just the stuff of fairy tales. Least I've never seen one. And say what you like, the ladies rather fancy me."

"No doubt, no doubt. But do tell, Marvin, have you narrowed the field down to one or two? Surely you can't keep all the local gnome girls pining for you, it would be too cruel to the lady gnomies."

"Sadly, the one for me is far away," said Marvin quietly. "Anna's her name, and she might not have me anyway. I've not seen her in years."

"When did you last see her?"

"When she was 13 and I was 12. Don't laugh," he scolded, catching a twinkle in Ty's eye.

"No, no, not at all, go on please."

"It was a magical moment. It will stay with me for life. I was no taller than your knee and standing on the very top of the ridge, a part we call the 'knife's edge,' with a sharp drop a few feet to either side and a narrow path down the middle. Anna suddenly appeared and came running toward me, her raven hair streaming and shining in the wind. I looked over my shoulder. Was she running to someone else? No, it was toward me!"

Marvin sniffled. "I'm sorry. This makes me very emotional. She'd never paid me much attention. Yet here she came, running faster and faster. I put out my arms to meet hers in an embrace, no doubt with a silly lovesick face. But, at the last second she launched herself, shoulder first, into my chest and knocked me to the ground. Immediately she turned her head back, with terror in her eyes, just as the sharp talons and shadow of a huge red-tailed hawk flashed over us and continued down the ridge."

"Wow," said Ty earnestly. "So she probably saved your life."

"Not 'probably.' Absolutely she did. And as she got up, she knew I was embarrassed. I could feel myself blush. But she just smiled, gave me a kiss on the forehead, leapt up, and was gone without a word. Then two weeks later she left with her family to live above ground, as 'topsiders'."

Ty arched his eyebrows in surprise and listened as Marvin poured out the rest of the story. Gnomes like any other civilization have varying beliefs, Marvin explained. Anna's parents had decided it was cowardly to live underground.

Her father, Hank, had begun arguing with cavern gnomes. "Are we men or moles?" Hank would demand.

"We go topside whenever we want," the cavern gnomes would argue.

"No you don't. You only go out when no biggies are around. Gnomes need to see the sun and stars overhead, not slink around in the shadows." And so would go the debate.

Then one day Anna and her parents set loose and weren't heard from again, Marvin said.

As the years passed, Marvin had persuaded himself that Anna was the love of his life. He begged his fellow gnomes to rack their brains for any clue Anna or her family might have given as to where they'd headed. But nobody could help and everyone grew tired of his questioning.

Finally, Marvin took to walking the back trails to the Hancock rail yard, where hobo gnomes gathered to camp and swap stories along the river before jumping the next freight train.

Finally, just a few weeks earlier, Marvin got his first good lead on Anna's whereabouts. Sitting around a fire, a wiry young gnome called "Fresno" told of a gnomish ranch he'd seen in Wyoming.

"Rubbish," objected one gnome. "That's too tall a tale. We hobos are all liars. Respect our intelligence for gnomes' sake."

"No, it's true," Fresno insisted. "Coming east I hopped a pickup truck at night as it pulled out of a roadhouse in Laramie. I'd nestled into the truck bed alongside a saddle, lariat, and fencing tools. A couple hours out, the driver fell asleep at the wheel."

"Was that was on the road between Laramie and Cheyenne, near the Jefferson National Monument?" the skeptical gnome asked.

"Trying to trip me up are you?" snorted Fresno. "It's a monument to Lincoln not Jefferson, a mosaic of rocks making up the body, regular sculpted head on top. Anyway, the driver started veering off the road, so I scampered on all fours up to the cab, threw open the back sliding window and yelled 'Wake up cowboy!' I knew I'd given myself away, and sure enough the cowboy wakes and pulls over to check the back. As he slowed, I leapt out with my bedroll and pack and ran up a dirt road in the dark."

Fresno explained he'd hid until the man left, then nestled down to sleep under a pine tree. The next morning he was stunned to awake to three gnomes astride Shetland ponies, the latter snuffling at his face. The three riders laughed at Fresno's wide-eyed look then quickly introduced themselves.

One was a gnome cowgirl, he said. At this the other gnomes laughed. "Oh please," one said, "you got the monument right but a cowgirl gnome? That's too much."

"What was her name?" Marvin asked in great excitement. "What was her name?"

"It was Anna," Fresno said. "Beautiful girl, great rider, and big brown eyes. She told me she was from back around here, near Warm Springs, West Virginia."

Marvin whooped, leapt over the campfire and gave Fresno a big hug. "Thank you, thank you," he cried.

"Okay, now stop your gob," a gnome had hissed from the darkness. "We're trespassing on private property, remember." At that Marvin had said his goodbyes and returned to the cavern.

"Wow," Ty said. "So now you're ready to set out on the road to find her. And what's the best clue you have for where to look?"

"I have no idea how far the family roams. All I know is that Fresno said the dirt road where he saw the family was called 'Happy Jack Road' in Medicine Bow National Forest off Interstate 80."

"Well, that's something to go on," Ty admitted. "Maybe we could make a road trip of it."

"Could we really? That would be fantastic! But you've got a girl of your own you're courting. How are things with Casey? The little gnomies think you're a prince and she's a princess. They demand bedtime stories about you and won't sleep until they've heard a good yarn."

Ty grimaced. "Nothing could be further from the truth, I'm afraid."

Ty told Marvin the sad story. Casey had a boyfriend in Baltimore. He'd given her his phone number but she hadn't called all week. He planned to visit Baltimore at the weekend and hoped he could stop by her house. If that didn't work, he'd try to see her when she returned to her cabin the following weekend. But even that didn't seem promising, as her boyfriend would be visiting then, too.

"I just know we clicked," Ty said in frustration. "I could feel it and she could, too. But she and this Vincent guy have been going out for a while and their families are old friends. But, these childhood romances don't last."

Ty noticed a stricken look on Marvin's face. "I'm sorry, Marvin," Ty added quickly. "Your case excepted. Cavern and cowboy gnomes stick together through thick and thin, I'm sure."

Marvin rolled his eyes. "I hope you do a better job keeping your foot out of your mouth around Casey. But go on."

"There's not much more to tell, unfortunately. And, I'm sorry Marvin, I didn't mean to sound skeptical about Anna." Ty said that in two weeks he would have a week off work, when Thurston would be out of town visiting family.

"That week I'll take you to Wyoming and we'll do everything to find Anna. Deal?" Ty stretched out his hand.

"Deal!" shouted Marvin, grabbing and shaking Ty's hand. Marvin was so excited, he dashed outside and did back springs once around the cabin with Midnight in pursuit.

"It will be great out on the road," Marvin said. "Maybe we can get a convertible like in that travel commercial with the biggie driving and the gnome riding shotgun. Oh, man that'd be great – no hiding, just cruising across America with the wind in our hair. Heck, all I'd have to do is sit real still and anyone on the road would think I was just a wood or plaster gnome. I'll wear my best tunic and britches, and cap. I'll be looking splendid when we roll into Wyoming."

For the remainder of the meal, Marvin told Ty excitedly about traveling gnomes. He told of gnome liberation in France, where biggies collected gnome statues from gardens and set them free in the woods. He told, too, of the popular biggie craze of traveling gnome pranks in which a biggie "borrows" a friend's gnome and takes him to exotic ports of call and sends photos back to the owner, showing the gnome luxuriating in the U.S. or abroad.

"How perfect," said Ty. "Biggies get to have some fun and gnomes stay true to their nature. Good fun all around."

Ty and Marvin had long since finished their dinner, and Marvin rose to leave.

"You know Ty," he said. "There's at least one thing that may get Casey looking for an excuse to see you."

Ty's face brightened. "Well, what is it," he demanded.

"It's us gnomes. Think about it, the world's pretty darn ordinary with just other biggies."

"Oh great," said Ty. "There I thought maybe you'd seen something in me a girl might like. But instead it's just my cool gnome friends. Gnomes are the new chick magnet? It's not puppies or babies any more but gnomes?"

CHAPTER 4

Ty worked for Thurston Tuesday through Friday. That week they built an old-school A-frame cabin to serve as a light-filled studio for a stained-glass artisan.

The structure went up fast – concrete piers for footers and a series of A-shaped rafters bolted together and set upright, with plywood sheathing tying it tight and sound.

By week's end it was fully enclosed, shingled, and weather tight. Finishing the interior would come later, after Thurston returned from vacation.

After work each day, Ty hiked up the mountain until he got a cell signal. He was disappointed to find Casey never called.

Each day, Ty also called Driveaway, the car delivery service, in which drivers have use of a car in return for transporting it long distance for the owner. Ty had an uncle who had used the company several times for cross-country trips but always between major cities.

Ty tried each day for a car to be driven from

Baltimore to anywhere in Wyoming or Colorado. He had not been optimistic, and from Tuesday until Thursday he had no luck. Friday came his break.

"We have a car that needs driving to Laramie, Wyoming," a cheerful operator told him. "It's a fun car, a classic Chevy Chevelle convertible. The owner requires that the driver have a perfectly clean driving record and agrees to drive the car no faster than 70 miles an hour. Can you meet both those conditions?"

Ty hesitated, delighted at the thought of how happy Marvin would be, riding in a convertible, the ultimate gnome machine.

"Sir?" the customer service agent said.

"Absolutely. That sounds terrific," Ty said eagerly. "I've restored classic cars with my dad. I know how to drive and maintain a car like that. I'll drive it just like it was mine."

Ty learned that the car's owner, James Carmichael, had a daughter, Amy, attending the University of Wyoming in Laramie. Amy was on an overseas exchange program for the summer, and would be flying directly to college for the start of the fall semester. Ty was delighted, knowing that Laramie was only 50 miles from where the hobo Fresno had seen Anna.

Ty had placed the call from a large flat rock on the ridge. When he hung up, he whooped and jumped up and down, then sat on the rock with his phone to thumb his way through the registration form.

Next he phoned his dad. "Dad," he said, "I'm coming home tomorrow and I've got a lot to report. Let me just tell you the basics real quick."

Ty told his father about Casey and how he hoped to see her in Baltimore. He also surprised him with the news that he'd arranged to drive to Wyoming to take a new friend to visit a family at their ranch, when he'd be idle with Thurston away.

"I'm all for it," Walt said. "An epic road trip with a friend or two is the best. Even better that you're on a quest."

Walt asked Ty how he'd return home after dropping off the car. Ty said he'd have to fly.

"I might need to borrow some money, Dad," he said. "I'd be able to pay you back after the next full week I work for Thurston."

"Not to worry, Ty," Walt said. "I'll buy you the ticket. The money's no more than I'd be paying to feed you at home. And, out in the mountains you're buying your own grub."

Ty laughed. "Well, if you put it like that, I won't argue."

Ty was grateful his dad hadn't asked who was accompanying him. He wasn't about to reveal his new gnome friends. No need to make my dad think I'm crazy, he figured.

"For my ride to Baltimore, I'm going to grab the Bayrunner shuttle that runs to Baltimore from Sandy's Truck Stop in Hancock," he said. "Thurston will drop me there on his way out of town. The shuttle drops off at the train station. From there, I'll take a cab to your place and fetch the car in the morning."

"Jeez, you've sure been busy," Walt said with a laugh.

"You don't know the half of it," Ty said, nodding.

"Meanwhile, is everything going well at home?"

"Yes, it is," Walt said. "Don't be shocked now but you may find I'm not home when you arrive. I'm getting my exercise and may be out for a run. So if you've just missed me and don't let yourself in, you might need to wait five or even ten minutes before I get back."

Ty laughed. "Wow, that's great, Dad, it really is. I can't wait to see you. Bye now."

Saturday morning Thurston dropped Ty off at Sandy's at 8 a.m. as planned. Having some time, Ty went into the restaurant and ordered a bacon-and-egg biscuit sandwich and a cup of coffee. He sat in a booth and looked out over the truck stop. In front were the gas pumps and beyond were several big rigs, the drivers sleeping in their cabs.

Soon an eight-passenger van lurched onto the lot, taking the ramp fast. The driver held the door for Ty who clambered aboard with a duffel bag, nodded to the passengers already aboard and nestled into a seat in the back.

"Next stop is Baltimore, gentlemen," the driver announced. "I'm a bit behind schedule but we'll make up the time easily, this early on a Saturday. Who's for snoozing and who wants the radio on?"

"Let me sleep, please," called one man. "Hard night last night."

"My vote's for sleep, too," said another.

Ty shrugged and looked out the window. To his right was the old B&O railroad line, long since turned into a biking and hiking trail. The sun glittered off the glass insulators on the poles along the old railbed.

In just a couple days, Ty thought, I'll be hurtling westward myself with a traveling gnome in the modern, hip gnome's favorite car, a big classic convertible, probably a first along this stretch. Unbelievable.

Who knows how many "biggies" may have had encounters with gnomes, Ty wondered. Trouble is no "biggie" is going to just start randomly asking around. Those who've never met gnomes will think you looney, maybe even get you committed. So, you can only make connections with other gnomes' biggie acquaintances through the gnomes themselves.

At 10 a.m., Ty arrived at the Amtrak station in Baltimore. He stepped out of the van and crossed over to the taxi stand. He pulled open the back door to the foremost cab and said "Brightside Road in Towson please. It's right near Robert E. Lee Park and Lake Roland."

"Sure, I know where you mean sir," the cabbie answered.

The drive took just 15 minutes along the Jones Falls Expressway, past urban row houses, industrial buildings, Druid Hill Park, and out into the affluent suburbs. They exited onto Ruxton Road and then looped south to Lake Roland.

Ty's heart raced as he realized they were but a few blocks from Casey's house. "Sir could you let me out right here please," Ty asked. "I'm going to a surprise party at a friend's house, and don't want to be seen pulling up in front."

Ty regretted the fib, but thought it easier than telling the whole story to the cabbie. He walked casually around the corner checking house numbers. Casey's address he'd memorized off Thurston's invoice book.

When he saw the matching house number, he was dismayed to see a sporty black BMW parked in front. That had to be the boyfriend's car. Rats, Ty thought to himself, what should I do now? What was I even thinking? Even if she'd been there alone, wouldn't he seem a bit creepy, like he was stalking her? Nothing good will come of this, he thought.

Ty started walking away. Two doors down the street he noticed a little garden gnome beneath a rosebush. On impulse, he jogged onto the neighbor's lawn, looked both ways, then produced a penknife, and quickly cut a large rose from the bush. He then snatched up the small gnome, jogged back to Casey's house, and placed the gnome and rose on her doorstep.

At that moment he heard Casey's and her father's voices, and saw the gate to the side yard start to open. He quickly crouched down and dashed around the far side of Vincent's car.

Please don't let them see me hiding here, Ty thought. That would be so embarrassing.

"What the heck is this?" he heard a boy ask.

"Very odd," Casey said, nervously.

"Well let's just go back on inside," Tim said. "I don't know what to make of it. Somebody's idea of a prank it seems – a gnome bearing flowers."

Ty groaned. That couldn't have gone any worse.

When all was quiet, Ty crouched and jogged down the line of parked cars until he was well out of view of the Bakers' house. He then walked briskly toward Lake Roland where he planned to disappear into a crowd, then find a cab to take him back to his dad's.

At the lake, he stopped to sit on a grassy hill overlooking the water. He was muttering to himself when a long shadow fell over him from behind. He looked back and was surprised to see Tim Baker standing there, dog at his side.

"I thought I might find you here," Tim said. "I knew you had to be close by with no cars on the street."

Ty blushed. "Good grief, I've sure made a fool of myself."

"Don't be too hard on yourself, Ty. I didn't come looking for you to embarrass you. I'm the one who's a bit embarrassed."

Ty looked puzzled. "You, why?"

Tim paused. "A dad probably shouldn't take sides in these things, but I'm worried about Vincent. He's been a good kid but has started misbehaving in various ways. Our two families are friends and Casey's caught in the middle."

"That puts Casey in a tough spot," Ty said.

Tim nodded. "It's awkward. Casey's torn and it's left you puzzled, too, obviously."

"How did she react to my silly little gnome and rose offering?" Ty asked, grimacing.

"She looked shocked and puzzled, wondering how it got there. I thought of you because you're the only guy other than Vincent she's spent any time with recently. I figured the gnome was some inside joke between you."

Ty shrugged innocently. "So where do I fit in, sir.

You came looking for me. Was it so I could help drive a wedge between Casey and Vincent? Or would you disapprove of me, too?"

"Too soon to tell Ty," Tim said, laughing. "Thus far you've made a good impression. You're well-mannered and work hard. That's a good start."

"I know I'm out of place in a rich part of town like this. But I've got excellent grades and am determined to get my education. I'm sure not going to end up running a bar like my dad and granddad."

"You show a lot of character," Tim said, extending his hand.

"Don't feel too sorry for me, sir. I manage to have some good fun, too. In fact, tomorrow I'm picking up a 1964 Chevy Chevelle convertible for a road trip to Wyoming."

Tim looked startled. "Get out, are you serious?"

"I am, and I wonder if you could give Casey a message from me? She'll have figured it was me with the rose and gnome. She knows I've fallen for her."

Ty asked Tim to tell Casey he was taking Marvin to Wyoming to find his lost love. Casey would remember Marvin. "We ran into him on the mountain and hung out a bit together. I expect she'll be intrigued to hear about that."

Ty paused. "And one more thing, please tell her it will be safe to pick up the phone when I call. I'll be far away and she won't need to worry that I'll drop by and make trouble between her and Vincent."

"That sounds like a great trip. And, yes, I'll tell Casey what you said – when Vincent's not around."

Ty hailed a cab home. He was pleased to find his

dad alone inside the bar. He was bus phoning in a keg order.

Walt held up a finger to say, I'll be with you in a minute.

Ty walked upstairs to wait, as he wasn't allowed in the bar, being a minor. Walt joined him shortly and gave him a hearty hug.

"Great to have you home. And look at you. I think you've already put on some muscle. What work has Thurston had you doing?"

Ty described the jobs he'd had. "It feels good, dad, it really does. We drive by that A-frame we built and I know that everything on that house is just right, from the concrete piers set level, the windows sealed right, the floors solid, everything done with precision. It's great to have something so tangible to show for your efforts."

"That does sound really good," Walt said with a sigh. "It must be a good change from the chaotic life you've had here."

"I've got no complaints. We've had some bad times but lots of good ones, too. And I've sure seen a lot for a kid my age. Can you get away for us to get a real dinner?"

"Sure, let's go."

Walt drove Ty to Mackey's Crab House, an old-timey place and local hangout, where "Baltimorons" sit with their hands crusted with Old Bay seasoning, cracking crabs with mallets on tables covered with Kraft paper.

"How often do you see this anymore?" Walt said. "People are just talking, enjoying each other's company and can't tap away on their phones because of all the crab and seasoning on their fingers."

Ty chuckled. "You go dad, I sense you working up to one of you back-in-my-day stories."

"Nah, I don't need to harangue you, not now. There you are out in the woods, without a cell signal, working with your hands, enjoying nature, meeting a great girl, the old-fashioned way no less, striking up conversation. Nope, I've got no problem with that at all. I'm downright proud of you. 'Casey' is her name, I recall. Tell me more about her."

"Alas, there's not much to tell since we spoke on the phone."

Ty recounted his disastrous trip to Casey's house and his chat with her dad. The only thing that gave him hope was Tim saying Casey looked stunned to see the gnome and rose. Ty wondered again how to interpret Casey's reaction.

"Earth to Ty," Walt said sharply. "You're not even listening to me. I'm starting to tell you about my new healthy life, hoping for encouragement and you're off in space."

"Sorry Pops, I'm all ears."

Walt spoke earnestly. "It started the very morning I drove you out to the mountains. For the first time in forever, I'd set an alarm and was up before you, cooking us that big breakfast. But before that I was disgusted to wake up and see I'd left the TV on and beer bottles lying around the apartment. I realized you'd been picking up after me each morning, hiding the truth of how slack I'd become."

After dropping Ty off at the cabin, Walt had taken

his time driving back to Baltimore. First he stopped at the swimming hole below the low-water bridge and took a swim in the cool, clean water. Next he drove across the bridge over the rail yard into Maryland and circled down to the Western Maryland Rail Trail. He'd put his wallet under the front seat, locked the van, and put the keys in the tailpipe.

He'd stretched and begun jogging on the paved, level trail, then sped up to the six-minute mile pace that he knew from his days as a high school distance runner. An out-of-shape man of 48, he had no illusions. He'd covered only about a quarter mile before he was gasping for air, and had to drop back to a gentle jogging pace. But he was thrilled nonetheless.

He'd hit the pace he wanted, his stride was as long as ever, and his legs felt strong. The endurance would come with time.

Walt would get his life back together, he resolved. And, he'd get out in the country more.

"I'm going to make you proud of me again," Walt said.

"Jeez Dad," Ty said. "We're going to wash the seasoning off the crabs with our tears. Enough of this. I've always been proud of you. You've always supported me. You've always been good to everyone around you. It's just yourself you need to take better care of. And now you're doing that, too? Great."

"I just never got over your mother leaving," Walt said with a sigh.

Ty shook his head. "Yeah, well she'd have stayed if you'd just stopped drinking downstairs. Start the self-pity again and you'll be right back boozing and backsliding, your big plans down the drain."

"True enough. But not to worry, Ty, I've turned the corner. I'm sure of it. I'm even thinking of selling the bar. I just need to figure out what to do next."

Ty smiled. "That's great, Dad. It really is. I hope you're serious."

"Speaking of the bar, we'd better get back. Jimmy's covering for me but he's all alone and I'm sure it's getting busy."

At nine the next morning, Walt drove Ty to pick up the Chevelle. The owner, James Carmichael, met them in the driveway and told them the history of the car.

"I picked it up cheap a couple years ago. It was in an old barn on a tobacco farm in Calvert County. The land was being cleared for a subdivision. The farmer's widow was thrilled at the price she got for her land, and sold me the car cheap. I trailered it home and got a local mechanic to get her running and roadworthy."

James said that at the time, his daughter had been underachieving in school and her grades were suffering. But she loved to drive the Chevelle. James offered her a deal. If she got straight A's her senior year in high school and first year in college, he'd give her the Chevelle.

"Of course," he said. "I thought she might go down the road to Towson State or somewhere else close by. Instead, she chose Wyoming. Well, I had to stick to my word, because she did her part. And I'd love to drive it out there myself but I've used up my vacation time at work."

"Well, not to worry, sir," Ty said. "I'll take very good care of her. You've got my word."

Soon Ty was behind the wheel, with the top down. He turned the key and the V8 jumped to life with a low rumble.

"Have a good trip, son," Walt said, waving as Ty pulled onto the street, headed for I-70 west.

CHAPTER 5

Ty raised his arm overhead and made one big sweeping wave to James and his father. As he turned onto the cross street, he took one last glimpse in the rear view mirror.

Next he heard a loud shriek. "Look out," yelled a small blurred figure in a Batman suit, diving head first through the handlebars of a pink bike and falling in his path.

"Good grief kid," yelled Ty. "Are you trying to get yourself killed?"

The figure jumped to its feet clearly unharmed, so Ty stole a quick look over his shoulder, relieved to see he was out of sight of Walt and James. He scrambled around front and looked at the half-pint Batman now executing deft karate chops in the air.

Batman grinned. "Give me some credit, lad. I'd hardly risk buggering up the trip. But there is a nosy lady watching us. Be a dear and pat me on the back, put my bike in the trunk, usher me into the front seat, and give the old lady a wave, will you. She'll think you're taking me home."

"You knucklehead, Marvin," hissed Ty. "What if she'd called the cops or an ambulance and they'd asked for identification. We tell them you're not an injured kid, just an everyday undocumented gnome? Think they'd just let us go? Hardly. Life's not all fun and games."

"For gnomes it sure is, thank heavens." Marvin said, picking up his pink bike and stowing it in the trunk. "Anyway, if you're done scolding, I've got a message for you."

"Well, what is it?" Ty asked.

"Casey says hi," Marvin said innocently, shooting Ty a look. "Said I should tell you that. So there you are."

"What?" Ty said, stunned.

"You missed that? Casey said hi. Should I drive for a bit? You seem distracted. We would make good time with me driving."

"Will you just get on with the story?" Ty begged, as they climbed into the car. "Or maybe I can leave you to ride to Wyoming as little Batman on the pink bike? You'd have a good conversation starter at least."

"Good point," Marvin said, nodding. "I'll tell you what happened."

"Thank you."

Marvin said that after Ty left for Baltimore, he'd realized just how enormously grateful he was to Ty. This must be the largest favor a biggie had ever done for a gnome, not that there were many, but still.

Marvin wondered how he might repay him. And, frankly, he'd hated the idea of missing any of the ride in the convertible.

So in a moment of inspiration, he'd shoved his Batman disguise and some other necessities in a knapsack and trotted down to the rail yard. What better place to begin his quest than the very spot he'd gotten his lead from kindly hobo Fresno?

Well, Baltimore was a straight shot east on the freight line, and Marvin had spent long enough in the hobo camp to study the technique for leaping aboard trains.

Trouble was, modern boxcars have stout slat siding, not at all like the ones in the old westerns and hobo movies, where a boxcar slowly rounds a bend with a handy grab bar and an open door. No, the best he could do was leap and scramble his way onto an open-top coal car, lie back, and grind out a filthy snow angel to anchor himself in place.

Fortunately, the ride to Baltimore took just an hour, time spent watching the clouds overhead, lest he move and send coal and himself, tumbling over the side. Once in town, he leapt off the coal car as it slowed entering a yard, and scampered down an embankment to a deserted street of ramshackle row houses.

Marvin quickly changed into his Batman suit and walked toward downtown. He stopped passersby to ask where he might find a Goodwill store. On the third try, a woman gave directions and stood staring after him as he walked off briskly, suspicious of the odd, costumed child with the deep voice and no parent in sight.

"Honey child, does your mama know where you

are?" the woman yelled after him. Marvin waved and
broke into a run.

Around 4 p.m. Marvin arrived at the Goodwill and
bought a girl's bike and began pedaling north, fussing
that a pink girl's bike is always the last one left.

Like Ty, Marvin had looked up the Bakers' address
in Thurston's invoice book left in his truck.

Marvin stood on the pedals as he rode, powering
quickly through the six miles north on Maryland
Avenue then onto North Charles Street and, finally,
Casey's street.

At that point, Marvin realized he had no plan. It
was pushing 6 p.m. and there he stood, astride the
pink bike, his cape gently fluttering in the breeze. The
sound of an approaching car spurred him into action.
Seeing no cars parked in front, he took a chance and
cycled fast into the Bakers' backyard. Looking up, he
examined the upstairs windows.

In one he saw a large teddy bear sitting on the
windowsill behind a gauzy curtain. Splendid, must be
Casey's room. More good luck, the curtain was
fluttering in the window. Yes, the sash window was
cracked to catch the breeze.

Marvin examined the metal straps and strong
masonry screws holding the downspout to the wall. A
professional job, capable of bearing his weight.
Grasping the downspout with both hands, he
clambered up easily.

What if he were to surprise Casey while she was
dressing? She might shriek. And what might she be
wearing, putting on, or taking off? Vexing, vexing.

"You think biggie children are easily distracted? For

gnomes it's much worse. We're forever distracted, off topic, putting humor ahead of duty. It's a curse, holds us back. It's why there's never been a gnome high school, university, physicist..."

Marvin paused in the narrative, noticing Ty looking more and more exasperated.

"Yes, on with story, not to worry," Marvin said.

Marvin had climbed the downspout, pulled off the bat hood and slowly raised his head to look over the ledge. There sat Casey by herself, sitting on a beanbag chair, wearing a t-shirt and sweatpants, carefully painting her toenails bright pink. A fetching shade, Marvin thought.

He ducked his head down. Better she hear my voice first before seeing my face, he figured.

"Casey," he'd hissed. "It's me, Marvin."

"What on earth?" Casey said, coming to the window and looking down nervously. Below she saw Marvin beaming up at her.

"It's a new era for gnomes," he said. "The gardens can't hold us."

"Moving up are you?" Casey asked. "Not into my bedroom you're not. Climb back down quick and meet me in the garage. The door's open. Get behind the freezer in the back, where you can't be seen from the street."

In a minute, Marvin was hunkered down in the garage and peeked out to see Casey walking toward him like a duck.

"Oh you're clever," hissed Marvin. "Walking funny to draw attention away from me. Masterful."

Casey shook her head. "No it's just the toe spreaders

girls use to paint nails easier, makes you have to walk on your heels. No teasing. So why are you here? And why are you taking such a risk? When we were on the mountain it was all hocus pocus. 'You have to wear the hood approaching the cavern, you have to come when it's completely dark, we have to be oh so secret.' But now, here you are in a big city dangling from window ledges in broad daylight?"

"It's vitally important, Casey, that's why. Ty really misses you, so do I and the other gnomes, especially the little gnomies. You're like family to us now, one of the biggies in our book along with our other great biggie friends Travis, Ty, Ms. Gallagher, etc. Plus we now officially honor our animal auxiliary Spike, Midnight, etc., not that they're quite on par yet. Have you heard anything from Ty? I know he wanted to contact you."

Casey told Marvin she'd seen the gnome and rose on her doorstep and heard from her father that Ty planned a trip to Wyoming, to help Marvin find Anna.

"Marvin that's so nice of Ty and so romantic of you," she said. "I wonder if a guy would ever do that for me."

"Of course we'll arrange it," said Marvin in delight. "We have lots of American dollars in our account. We could buy you an aeroplane ticket to Wyoming. Then you could hide and Ty could look for you while I look for Anna. What fun. I'm sure he would look very hard. Very romantically, too. Maybe calling out for you in poems."

Casey laughed. "Maybe he would. But he doesn't even know me very well. We only hung out together one day, though I admit it was probably the most memorable day of my life, between him and the gnomes. Until I saw you today, I'd almost persuaded myself it was all just a dream."

"So, do you have a message I can tell Ty? Please make it a happy making message but still truthful."

"Please tell him I said 'Hi'," Casey said with a smile.

Marvin grinned. "I'll tell him you said 'Hi', and that when you did, you had a wide smile with dimples, and that you dipped your chin and pushed back your hair." I think he would like to know that. "'Coyly,' could I say that? Or is that a word just in books?"

"No, that's a good word. You can use it outside of books. You have some charm, Marvin. I wish you good luck finding Anna."

Marvin paused in relating his visit with Casey and looked at Ty.

"Alright!" said Ty with a big smile of his own. "Not a weak smile but a smile with dimples. Not much, but that's something." He reached over, and rubbed his knuckles playfully over Marvin's Batman hood. "You're a good gnomie. So, what happened next?"

"I said goodbye, got my Batman costume back on and rode down to the Chesapeake Tavern. I wanted to see if I could talk just to you secretly and sleep somewhere without your dad or anyone else knowing I was there. But weren't nobody home."

Marvin paused and fidgeted before continuing. "I was a little bad, I'm afraid. I climbed up the back wall, pushed open a window and looked in your bag. I found the address for picking up the car. I studied that, then went and slept on a metal ledge under a railroad bridge. Some people were living there and were throwing bottles and telling naughty stories. I listened for a while then fell asleep. Then this morning I rode my bike to Mr. Carmichael's house to surprise you."

"That's alright," Ty said. "Everything worked out. And I am glad you talked to Casey. I was worried she would be mad at me for turning up at her house without being invited. From what you say, it sounds like she's not."

Ty looked over to see Marvin was distracted, running his hands across the dashboard. Ty followed Marvin's eyes, glancing back and forth between the road and the car's interior. It was definitely old school, lacking many of the refinements and safety features of contemporary cars.

In front were well-stuffed vinyl seats without side bolsters, no head rests, and only lap belts. The look was more like an old-fashioned, raked-back barber's chair than a modern car seat. The shifter was on the floor in a long chrome channel. The dash was chromed around the instrument cluster, as were the window handles. The doors were upholstered in plush velour.

Rounding out the interior was an oversized thin steering wheel, allowing for the one-handed cruising style discouraged by today's driving instructors, but immediately adopted by Ty for authenticity's sake.

The top down, Marvin was beside himself with glee as Ty revved the engine up an on ramp onto I-70, their first taste of highway driving in the glorious Chevelle convertible. As the car settled in at the 65 mph speed limit, the engine emitted a low, steady rumble.

"Wow, it doesn't shimmy, shake, or rattle," Ty said, delighted. "What a great car."

Soon they were rolling through Frederick and Hagerstown, and eyed the vast 800-foot-deep Sideling Hill cut.

"We'll be running through there ourselves in just a couple hours, after we load up," said Ty, turning off the highway and onto the 340 bridge across the Potomac River, through Warm Springs and Little Falls. Soon they were over Lonesome Mountain and back to Travis' cabin.

Marvin patted Midnight, then rushed uphill to the cavern to pack his things. Ty packed and took a walk with Midnight, who was very happy to see Ty after the night alone.

Marvin reappeared about an hour later, trudging down the hill with a leather pack on his back, bobbing side to side with each step. He and Ty loaded their gear in the car, while Midnight stood on the porch, looking on anxiously.

"C'mon boy," Ty yelled. "Of course you're coming. Who knows when we'll next have a chance to visit Wyoming?"

Midnight barked, leapt off the porch, and bounded toward the car, leaping high in the air."

"Yikes, the paint," said Ty, cringing. But, fortunately, Midnight easily cleared the side of the Chevelle, landed in the middle of the back seat, and flopped down, thumping his tail. Ty locked the cabin, then he and Marvin took their seats and returned to the freeway and headed west.

"Let's see if we can make Wheeling, West Virginia, tonight," Ty said. "It's about 180 miles on I-68 so we should get there by 10 p.m., figuring in an hour's stop for dinner and gas.

Marvin beamed with glee. "Anna, your gnome boy is coming. Soon no more lonely cold nights in the mountains for you."

"Oh Ty," he added, "Casey gave me an idea for a nice present. Very girlie thing. It spreads your toes for painting. Is that very romantical?"

"It's a nice start," Ty said. "I should buy something for Casey in Wyoming."

As they talked, Ty smiled at how easily the Chevelle tackled the long upgrade through Sideling Hill and on through the rugged country toward Cumberland.

Ty asked Marvin whether the gnomes studied geography. Martin told them that geography was considered a very dangerous subject for gnomes. The trouble was, with gnomes being so impulsive, learning about all the exciting places they could visit would encourage them to run away from home.

"Well since you are already on the loose, how about you read up and teach both of us about the country we're traveling through?"

Ty said that being on the freeway they would have good cellular service the whole way to Wyoming. "So, you can read in the car as we go. The next city is Cumberland. See which you can find out about that."

Marvin started busily pecking away once Ty had explained how to use a web browser. He discovered that Cumberland was the end of the Chesapeake and

Ohio Canal, a gateway for westward migration through the Cumberland narrows.

"Oh," Said Marvin, "The Internet says we must stop at the Queen City Creamery. It has wonderful ice cream."

"We can get ice cream with dinner. We should keep going so it's not too late when we stop for the night."

"But the Internet says we must stop. Is it okay to disobey the Internet? And ice cream is very yummy. I only get it when I wear my bat cape into the store at Little Falls. But at home it is not handmade fresh right there at the store. Maybe we should obey the Internet."

Ty promised Marvin that the Internet would tell them to stop at another ice cream restaurant, which they did at Pappy's in Uniontown, Pa., where Marvin was ecstatic about his upside-down banana split.

"Where do biggies think they go when they die? Do they think there will be ice cream there like upside-down banana split? If so, I would like to visit there, maybe later go back to where gnomies go. Gnomes don't agree on where they go when they die. They fight about it."

"Biggies are the same way, trust me," Ty said.

They rolled into Wheeling after dark.

Marvin had been studying. "Ty, the Internet is very exciting about Wheeling. There was a Fort Henry where there was much fighting. There a Major McCullough was being chased by Indians and on his horse leapt 300 feet down Wheeling Hill to escape."

Marvin paused. "That sounds too brave for a biggie. Probably he was a gnome. And maybe a gnome cowboy like Anna. Maybe Anna can lend me a horse so I can be a famous hill leaper like McCullough and the Internet will write about me and Anna will see I am a good cowboy, too."

"Marvin, I think you should read what the Internet says about being a cowboy. Mostly it is raising, feeding, and selling cattle and other livestock. To make a good impression on Anna you should say you want to raise animals, not jump off tall hills."

"You know, Ty, I hope Anna will want to come back home to Lonesome Mountain with me. The grand cavern is much nicer now than when she left and we are selling many nice wood gnomes, have a good school in the cavern, and have new biggie friends like you. I think she will like it. But I will stay on the ranch with her if she wants me to do that."

"Be patient, Marvin. Give it some time to see how you like it in Wyoming and don't try to rush her into deciding to move back to Lonesome Mountain. First you have to find her anyway. We need a plan and supplies for that."

Ty found a roadside motel where the three of them spent the night and enjoyed a generous free breakfast the next morning, the cook giving Ty some sausage links as a treat for Midnight.

The next day they drove 510 miles to Springfield, Illinois. Marvin said Springfield was first settled by European Americans in the late 1810s, around the time Illinois became a state. The most famous past resident was Abraham Lincoln, who lived in Springfield from 1837 until 1861, when he went to the White House as president.

"Wow," said Ty when they stopped to visit Lincoln's home in Springfield. "Lincoln really traded up from his one-room pioneer cabin he had in Kentucky. Look at this, 20 rooms, two stories, and two fireplaces."

After a night in a local motel, they drove 425 miles from Springfield to Omaha, Nebraska, on the Missouri River, where they stopped at Lewis and Clark Landing.

Marvin was impressed. "The Internet says Thomas Jefferson made the Louisiana Purchase, buying a huge amount of land. He then sent Lewis and Clark with 43 other men to explore the country he bought, all the way from the Mississippi to the Pacific Ocean. They camped here for four days during their trip."

Marvin was very excited about Lewis and Clark. As a park ranger recounted the history, Marvin stood toward the back of the crowd in his Batman suit acting out the stories told.

He strained at an imaginary wooden boat, pulling it upstream. And when the ranger told of the Lewis and Clark party's steady need to hunt for food, Marvin got on all fours and rushed back and forth among the bewildered tourists. Intermittently, he'd crumple and twitch as if he were an antelope shot by hunters.

After the walk and ranger's talk, Martin was still very excited about Lewis and Clark. He begged Ty to take him to a store to buy camping gear.

"I'll need the gear later anyway when I'm sleeping out in the mountains looking for Anna. And this way we can both sleep out to practice. We can sleep right down here by the water where Lewis and Clark did."

Ty found a Megamart where they bought sleeping

bags, air mattresses, a small green nylon pup tent, cookware, flares, paper, plastic paper protectors, markers, tacks, string, canned food, dog food, bottled water, and a cheap cellphone with prepaid minutes. They then went back to Lewis and Clark Landing, where they parked and scrambled down to a secluded spot on the river to pitch their tent.

Marvin was excited and it took him a long time to get to sleep. He had been talking about all the sights they'd seen on their trip, and seemed like he was getting tired. But then he was suddenly seized with a thought.

"Ty you might teach me some cowboy songs. The Internet told me that real cowboys sometimes make fun of new cowboys. They call them dudes and city slickers. But I want to be like a real cowboy, the kind you see in a movie."

"Okay," said Ty, wearily. Let's start with "Home on the Range."

The song went passably well, Ty thought, and would be a nice end to the day.

Marvin, though, was stroking his chin, thinking hard. "Wait, Ty, the Internet says there are many more great songs from the west. We should sing *Camptown Races* and *My Darling Clementine*. Casey said I had charm. Singing would be extra charm, right?"

They were up early the next morning, knowing they had a 530-mile drive ahead. Marvin was especially animated.

"Today's the big day, Ty," he said. "Today we arrive at Anna's cowboy land. Do you remember the name of where we are going? I like that name and the story."

"Yes, it's a great name. The road we turn onto is called Happy Jack Road in Medicine Bow National Forest. Did you see what the Internet had to say about how it got its name?"

"Yes, I asked the Internet after you went to sleep. I asked so many things there is a red bar on the phone when the Internet needs more electricity." Marvin looked worried.

"Not the whole Internet, Marvin. It's just the phone that needs electricity and we can get some through the cigarette lighter plug in the dashboard right in the car."

"Okay, that's good. Anyway Happy Jack was a logger who lived there about 120 years ago. Happy Jack was not his real name. It is a nickname he got because he was always singing while he worked."

"That's a good story Marvin. You know what you need to do next is make signs. Then you should also ask the Internet how to find cattle using a dog. You can try searching for 'teaching a dog to track' or 'tracking cattle.'"

Ty and Marvin spent the remainder of the drive working out the details of how to hunt for Anna and her family. First Marvin made signs, for which they reluctantly raised the Chevelle's convertible top, agreeing it was no good having the signs fly out the back, carried on the wind.

Marvin wrote signs with great enthusiasm. "Anna will you marry me?" he wrote on the first one.

"Keep that one for later, I'd say," said Ty.

"Hi Anna, it's Marvin from WVa., Meet me here,"

Marvin tried.

"Better," said Ty. "But if you put those up all over, you won't know where to wait for her."

"Hi Anna, it's Marvin from WVa. Meet me at sunset at the Hwy & Happy Jack Rd," he wrote.

"Yes, that's perfect," said Ty.

Marvin made many of these signs, writing with a marker, inserting the sheets in plastic sheet protectors to protect them from wind and rain.

Next he read up on teaching a dog to track.

"It's too bad we didn't teach Midnight to track when he was a puppy," Marvin said. "That's when they learn the best."

"I don't think we'll have too hard a time with Midnight. Remember he's spent his whole life living in the woods and he spent weeks finding his own food after Grandpa Travis died. We just need to make him understand that we're looking for live cattle and not, say, dead prairie dogs."

"Yes, there is no reason to think that just because we find a dead prairie dog, that Anna will be there, too. Good point."

After some intense study, Marvin was certain he knew how to train Midnight. The trick was to find either some cattle dung or cattle hair and have Midnight sniff it. Then one of them would drop little bits of dung or hair out in the grass along with dog food, not on top of the dung, of course. That way Midnight would learn that it was a fun and rewarding game for him to follow the trail of the cow scent and then get dog treats, too.

"Dogs really love this, the Internet says. They like to

feel useful and to please their owners, plus they like to exercise their excellent sniffers, work hard, and find things. And when they get doggie treats, too, it makes it almost the best fun a dog can have."

Ty agreed this sounded very promising. "Remember, too, that you've got the flares," he said. If you want to try them, you can put out signs saying 'Anna, find me by my flare at nine tonight.'"

Ty said altogether Marvin and Midnight would have three ways to find Anna. They could pick up the trail of the cows' scent. She could find them at the meeting places written on the signs. And she can find them by the flares.

Ty paused. "You know what we've forgotten? We've spent this whole trip learning about old McCollough, Abraham Lincoln, and Lewis & Clark. But we've forgotten modern communications. You've got a phone. She can just call you if you put your number on the signs, too."

Marvin slapped his forehead and nodded. Then he picked up his marker and went back to work.

The trio arrived at the turn for Happy Jack Road just as the sun was beginning to set. A short distance from the junction, Ty pulled the Chevelle off onto the shoulder and surveyed the country while Marvin and Midnight ran over to water a solitary pine tree.

The land was gorgeous and wide open, with rolling hills and stands of pines on high ground. Interspersed throughout were dramatic red and brown stone bluffs that invited climbing to take in the stunning views seen through the clear mountain air.

The land was covered with tall prairie grass waving

in the gentle wind. It seemed perfect country for Anna's family. The grasses were tall enough for gnomes to hide easily, and the hillocks and stone bluffs had undulating bases, making little coves where it would be easy to shelter livestock.

They slept well in their tent off Happy Jack Road. Perhaps the new smells fired Midnight's imagination. Whatever the reason, he was woofing and twitching in a dream when Ty woke.

Ty stretched, crawled out of his sleeping bag and built a small, hot cooking fire on which he brewed coffee and cooked eggs and sausage. This was the last fresh breakfast there'd be for a while, as they had no ice.

Marvin and Midnight awoke to the sounds and smells of cooking and happily shared in the breakfast feast.

Afterwards, the three of them stood by the side of the Chevelle. Marvin patted the fender fondly.

"It's a great thing you've done for me," Marvin said. "You've helped me look for Anna and you've showed me a lot of great country and history."

He paused. "It's a good thing gnomes never cry," he added, a tear welling in one eye.

"Yes," said Ty. "That wouldn't do at all." The three shared a man, gnome, dog hug.

"This would make a great buddy movie," said Marvin. "We have a road trip and adventure and maybe girls."

"Yeah. That last part we're still working on," said Ty, climbing into the car. "Marvin, be sure to save your phone battery. Call only when you have big news.

Turn it on once a day to check for messages. Then turn it off again. Okay?"

Marvin nodded and Ty walked toward the car. Midnight bounded after him and braced himself to jump into the rear seat.

Ty kneeled and placed a hand on his back. "Midnight, you need to stay here with Marvin and use your sniffer to help him."

Meanwhile, Marvin came trotting over with his pack full of supplies and some tufts of cow hair he'd found on tree bark, where a cow had scratched itself.

He held the hair under Midnight's nose. "Use your sniffer, doggie, find those cattle. Midnight put his nose to the wind and charged off, with Marvin In pursuit."

Ty watched and chuckled, noting that in the tall grass often all that was visible was Midnight's tail and the pointy top of a gnome hat, Marvin having become a topsider, wearing gnome attire in public.

"Bye now."

CHAPTER 6

Ty drove the nine remaining miles to the University of Wyoming in Laramie. He parked on the street and walked to the campus' historic Prexy's Pasture, used originally for grazing livestock but now ringed by campus buildings.

Ty sat on a bench and called Amy Carmichael, who was eager to take delivery of the Chevelle and delighted the car had made the trip without trouble.

She gave Ty directions to her townhouse and arranged to meet him there at 10 a.m. after biology class.

This gave Ty time alone to call Casey. She answered on the first ring. It was that easy. Ty was stunned.

"Ty, is that you?" Casey asked, puzzling at the unfamiliar number.

"Yes, yes it is. It's so great to hear your voice. I've been so looking forward to talking to you again."

"Me, too," Casey said happily.

"So Marvin came to see you? I couldn't believe it when he told me. I didn't ask him to put in a good word for me, honest. I was as shocked as you were."

Casey laughed. "Maybe not quite as shocked. You didn't have a hairy gnome climb up to your bedroom window. But he was good company and a very devoted friend to you. I was touched."

"So," Casey added, "How was the trip to Wyoming? What all did you see along the way? And how did you keep people from noticing you had a gnome riding with you, for goodness sakes?"

"Mostly he wore his Batman outfit, pretending to be a kid. And you know being childlike comes naturally to gnomes."

"I'll say."

Ty took a deep breath, anxious about what he was about to say. "Casey, I've got so much to tell you about the trip, and you're the only one I can tell the story to without being thought crazy. Can you come meet me at the airport, then drive me home? I'll buy you dinner on the way. And, I won't put any moves on you, unless you insist. Honest."

Casey laughed. "Okay, it's a deal."

Ty could barely keep the excitement out of his voice as he gave her his flight number and said goodbye.

He hung up, leapt to his feet, and pumped a fist in the air.

"A good phone call, I'd guess," said an oncoming college girl walking with a friend.

"I just got a date with a girl who rivals you two beauties," Ty said with a grin. "Imagine that."

"You're well out of your league then," said the second girl with a straight face, to which they all burst out laughing.

"Good luck," they shouted as Ty waved and jogged

off to the student union. There he found the phone number of the shuttle bus to Denver International Airport, reserved a seat and was soon on his way after dropping the Chevelle with Amy Carmichael. "Take it quick," he'd told her. "Don't tempt me to drive it off."

Thoughts whirled in Ty's head as he looked out the bus window reliving the past few hours, in which he'd left behind Midnight, Marvin, and the Chevelle, arranged a dinner date with Casey, and soon would retrace his tiring, almost week-long journey with a flight of just four hours.

Ty made his plane easily and dozed fitfully for most of the flight, tired but also apprehensive at seeing Casey. What if she changed her mind and didn't show, he wondered.

But he needn't have worried. He exited the United plane and walked briskly up the jet way to the terminal at BWI Airport. There Casey stood, smiling and waving, looking pretty and relaxed in a t-shirt and shorts.

They exchanged an awkward hug, then pulled apart, looking ill at ease.

"Let's try that again," Ty said, reaching an arm around her waist and pulling her sharply toward him.

Casey yelped in surprise. "Easy there cowboy. You've spent too much time alone on the range. Let's find somewhere to eat and you can tell me about your adventures. How about a burrito at Baltimore harbor?"

"Sure, that would be great. I've been eating camping chow the past couple days and a fresh burrito would sure hit the spot."

Soon they were sitting down to eat, looking out through plate glass windows at the harbor and Baltimore Aquarium.

Before starting her meal, Casey pushed her long hair back behind her ears and looked up at Ty, who was staring at her transfixed.

"Good grief, stop staring and eat your meal will you," Casey said, jolting Ty out of his daze.

"Sorry, I'll get over it, I'm sure. And don't get all full of yourself. I admit I was thinking how great you looked. But keep in mind that the only two faces I've seen for the past week have been a drooling black lab and lumpy nosed hairy gnome. On the other hand they weren't scolding me either, so they had that plus."

"Alright, alright," Casey said, smiling. "So tell me all about the trip."

Ty related the trip's adventures through leaving Marvin and Midnight with their various supplies on Happy Jack Road. Casey quizzed Ty about how Marvin and Midnight would conduct their search.

"Well, given that the whole gnome thing is so farfetched, this piece doesn't seem any crazier than anything else. I guess it could work," Casey said, a little doubtfully.

"I tell you what," Ty said. "I told Marvin to turn on his phone briefly each evening at 6 p.m. When we're done here, let's find a quiet spot outside where we can call him."

Casey agreed and the two were silent for a moment.

"So," Ty said, trying to sound casual, "are you and Vincent still planning to go out to Little Falls next weekend?"

Casey nodded.

"It would kill me to know you're there and not have a chance to see you. Is there some way we can get together, even just briefly?"

"I don't see how we could."

"Does Vincent even know I exist?" Ty pleaded. "He wouldn't be suspicious of me and I would be perfectly well behaved."

Casey shook her head. "No, I've never mentioned you to Vincent. But I doubt you'd be behaved. And even if you were, I'd worry about Vincent. He can be very possessive."

"I'll bring a friend and we can go canoeing. Thurston will go. His canoe got busted last winter by a falling tree and he's been eager to get out on the water. Uncle Travis has two canoes. You and Vincent can be in one canoe and Thurston and I will be in the other. You can just introduce us as what we are – a handyman and his helper who are family friends."

"Yeah, except the helper barely knows me but has a huge crush on me, probably because, as he so nicely put it, I'm the only girl for miles around."

"I do, too, know you. I know things about you we've never talked about. There are things I can just tell. I'll prove it."

Ty reached for his paper burrito bag and pulled a pen from his pocket. "I'm going to write some things down here," Ty said. "This will take me a minute or two."

Casey watched, intrigued, as Ty alternately wrote, stroked his chin, and took deep breaths. "Jeez, don't strain yourself," she said, chuckling.

Finally he stopped and folded the paper into a roll, blank side in, so only one line of text showed at a time.

"Okay," he said. "I'm going to ask you questions about yourself. You tell me your answer, read my answer, and award points for correct answers. Okay?"

Casey nodded, smiling. "You keep things interesting handyman, I'll give you that."

She picked up the paper and read aloud. "What do I want to be in life? Casey's answer: be a teacher. Ty's answer: try to save the world, probably something with kids." Casey nodded. "One point for Ty."

"What do you prefer, being around people like yourself or meeting people from all different backgrounds? Casey's answer: all different backgrounds. Ty's answer: all different backgrounds. Second point for Ty."

"Do you prefer to read books or watch TV? Casey's answer: read books. Ty's answer: read books. Third point for Ty."

"How important is it to you to exercise and lead a fit, healthy lifestyle? Casey's answer: very important. Ty's answer: very important. Fourth point for Ty."

"How important is it to you to be thought a goddess by Ty and gnomies young and old? Casey's answer: not important. Ty's answer: vitally important. No additional point for Ty."

Ty laughed. "I think you weren't honest about the goddess question but I'll let it slide."

"Alright," Casey said, "you do know me pretty well. But tell me what good you think it will do for us to get together with Vincent paddling down the river in separate canoes. What's that do for anyone?"

"Well, canoeing is invigorating. It's exciting paddling the rapids and avoiding downed trees. We'll see bald eagles, hawks, fish jumping, maybe a local gal in a tied off t-shirt and Daisy Dukes. That's all good."

"Nice image for you I'm sure. How about you answer the question?"

"Okay, here's the answer. I want to see you and Vincent together. If I see you two have the rapport and respect that we do, then I'll bow out. But if not, I'm going to keep trying to win you over. I'll stop if you tell me to but won't just give up and regret it later."

Casey stared at Ty in silence for a few moments. "Wow you don't mince your words, Ty."

"Look, I'm realistic. We're still high school kids. I know the odds are against us. But I need to know." Ty suddenly smiled and waved at a puzzled looking girl behind the counter. "And in case it doesn't work out, I did score a phone number off the girl at the register."

"Okay," Casey said. "Against my better judgment, Vincent and I will come canoeing with you and Thurston or another friend of yours. Just don't show up alone. Deal?"

"Deal," said Ty eagerly.

"Frankly Ty," she said. "I'm curious to see how things go with Vincent myself. They haven't been so great recently."

"I'm devastated to hear that," Ty said with a huge grin. "Devastated."

"Oh jeez, I should never have told you that."

"Not to worry. Really. I will be on my best behavior.

I promise you."

They finished their dinner and Casey drove Ty home.

"Wow," she said, parking the car in front of the Chesapeake Tavern. "How authentic. No yuppie fern bar here, I'd say."

Ty grimaced. "Yeah, not the best place for a kid growing up either. But I've sure seen and learned a lot here. And there have been lots of role models here – good ones and bad ones."

"Coming through and don't let me have a beer," rang out loudly as Ty and Casey stood talking outside the tavern. "Saw you pull up."

"That's my dad," Ty said laughing and pointing at a man running toward them from twenty yards away. "Pops, I'm very impressed. You really are getting in shape. And that's a darn good pace. Or is this all a setup? Were you just hiding up the block so you could start sprinting when we passed?"

"Show some respect for your elders," Walt said, still breathing hard. "And who is this lovely friend of yours?"

"This is Casey," Ty said.

"Oh," said Walt. "Ty told me about you, that you're Tim Baker's daughter. I met your dad some years back. So we're almost neighbors out in West Virginia. It's very nice to meet you. I'll be driving Ty out to Little Falls tomorrow morning. Ty was saying he's looking forward to seeing you out there again this summer."

Ty blushed. "Thanks dad."

"He's been telling me the same thing sir," Casey

said. "I've told him I have a boyfriend but he's very persistent. It's a bit awkward."

"It would be nice if you wouldn't talk about me like I'm not even here," said Ty. "Casey, let me walk you to your car."

Ty led Casey to her car and opened the door for her. She climbed into the driver's seat. "Please don't be mad at me Ty," she said. "I'm trying to be a friend to you without leading you on. I know it's difficult. Let's see how things go when we meet up out on the river."

"Yes, that will help sort things out," Ty said. "See you soon." Casey smiled, waved and drove away. Ty stood a few seconds after she turned the corner, then climbed the stairs to the apartment.

Ty and his dad watched some TV together afterwards, then went to bed early so they could enjoy a long day together out in Little Falls. Driving out, they stopped at a little Amish market in Hagerstown, where they loaded up with fresh vegetables, meat, and cheese.

It was a hot, muggy day, too hot for hiking, so they went tubing instead. Travis, ever thrifty, had a couple of much-patched truck inner tubes that Ty and Walt launched from the first low water bridge.

The water was clear and cool with many small bass jumping around rocks and in the weed beds along the river. There was much other wildlife to see, too. Turtles sunning themselves on fallen logs, dove into the water at their approach. A deer bounded down the steep westward slope and ran easily across the shallow river, disappearing into the brush on the other side.

Ty and his dad laid on their backs, finding their

speed matched the eastward course of the clouds overhead. As they floated along, they were passed by a man and his young son each paddling kayaks laden with camping gear.

"Where'd you put in?" Walt called to them.

"Up at Capon Bridge on US 50," the dad replied.

They were on the third day of their river trip, he said. They had camped each night along the river and were headed to the confluence with the Potomac River, where the boy's mother would pick them up for the ride home.

"Remember how we used to take trips like that with Grandpa Travis?" Walt asked. "That was a heck of a lot of fun, sitting around hearing him tell those old yarns of his."

Walt chuckled. "How could I forget? He used to tell some crazy tall tales. For instance, do you remember when he used to talk about seeing gnomes in the woods?"

"Gnomes," gasped Ty. "Did he really say he saw gnomes?"

"It was strange," Walt said. "He'd say that one moment, sounding serious. And the next moment he would say something mysterious like 'Or maybe I was mistaken.' It was one of his many little quirks but immensely funny to him somehow."

Ty and his dad lazed in their tubes and enjoyed the quiet for a while.

Walt then paddled closer to Ty so he could be heard over the sound of the riffles. "I felt bad last night. That girl Casey seemed great – beautiful, smart, funny, someone you shouldn't be ashamed to bring home to meet your dad. No doubt she lives in a nice big house in the cool, leafy suburbs and comes to see your dad living above a bar, broken down cars, trash on the street, heat shimmering off the asphalt. That can't make the best impression."

"Not to worry," Ty said. "You've been a great dad to me. And all the stuff I've seen down there has taught me a lot."

"Don't be too intense now and scare Casey off."

"I'm walking a tightrope, Pops. I'm crazy about that girl and struggling not to pursue her too hard nor let her get away. Plus, her boyfriend's coming here this weekend."

"Boyfriend, ouch."

"Not to worry dad, I'm going to steal her away. If things were going great with him, she'd never have spent the time she has with me."

"Well, best of luck. You're due to catch a break."

They soon finished their tubing run and climbed the river bank to a dirt road, along which they walked back to Walt's van, stopping to eat wild wineberries and blackberries.

Back at Travis' cabin they barbecued burgers and ate corn and peaches Walt had bought from a farm stand in Hancock. After dinner they sat chatting on the front porch watching the fireflies flash in the dark over a small meadow next to the river.

"Well, I'd better be getting back," Walt said. "Have fun working with Thurston this week."

"Oh, I will dad. It will be good to stay in one place and just work for a week."

Walt waved goodbye and Ty turned and walked into

the cabin. He felt a bit lonely without either Midnight or Marvin around. He turned in early and walked over to Thurston's first thing in the morning."

"Well, well," said Thurston meeting Ty in the driveway. "Who have we here? Are you ready to get to work?"

Ty grinned. "What do you have for us today Thurston?"

"Ever laid laminate flooring?"

"Nope."

"You're going to love it. It's new construction up the mountain, perfectly level, clean subfloor. The flooring snaps together at the ends and sides. You stagger the pieces, lay each row up to the last one and snap it in, then on to the next. Plus, the house already has AC running."

"Man that sounds great," Ty said, his shirt already sticking to his back from the heat.

"And to really spoil you, I brought you a pair of foam kneepads. "Makes a big difference over the course of a full day."

"Terrific, thanks. How was your vacation?"

"Relaxing, just hanging out with family and friends."

"Yours?"

"Fun, I gave a friend a lift to Wyoming in a '64 Chevy Chevelle convertible. Midnight went along, too, for a nice doggie vacation," Ty said, laughing. "First trip out west for all of us."

"What?" Thurston said, his mouth hanging open. As they clambered into the truck and drove to the job site, Ty recounted the trip, detailing the sights and stops but staying vague about the friend who'd accompanied him.

"Just a guy chasing an old flame," he said. "He doesn't drive well, so I took him."

"Good grief, you did all that driving for a friend?" Thurston said. "And you're how old, not even eighteen?"

"That's right. I'll be eighteen next April. I caught a break in them letting me drive the car at my age. The owner had to sign off on it. Great guy though, and the car handled the trip just great. I babied it the whole way, checking fluids, parking it away from other cars, etcetera."

Thurston's account of the floor-laying job was correct. The work was comfortable, clean, and efficient. The only tough part was the continual kneeling and standing back up. Ty felt the soreness after work when hoisting Travis' fiberglass canoe on his shoulders and carrying it down to paddle in the river.

He sighed with relief as he lowered one end of the canoe to the ground on a gravel boat ramp and rolled it right side up.

"Hey there," a girl's voice called from the woods to one side.

"Hi," Ty said, turning and seeing a slim brunette kneeling beside a kayak under a huge sycamore tree. "You startled me. I didn't see you there."

"I'm having trouble with my kayak paddle," she said, peering into the shaft of one piece. "I pushed down the locking pin so I could put the two halves together. But the pin got torqued over to the side, and won't pop back up so I can't lock the pieces together. Do you have a pocket knife or any other tools with you? I'd use my keys but I hid them in my tailpipe at the takeout."

"Let me have a look," Ty said, and squinted into the hole in the shaft. "Yep, that's exactly what you need, a nail or a thin Phillip's head screwdriver. I've got tools up at my cabin. I have to go back for my paddle, cooler, and life jacket anyway. Do you want to wait here? I'll be right back."

"I'll keep you company, and help you carry your gear. You must be tired from carrying the canoe, I can at least give you a hand."

"Sure," said Ty, meeting her look. "I'd be happy for the company. I'm living here alone for the summer working construction and don't have anyone to talk to outside of work. I'm Ty. What's your name?"

"Lisa, I'm just here for the summer working, too."

"Really, whereabouts?" Ty asked, as they started up the hill.

"I'm teaching acting and improv at The Art Haus in Warm Springs."

"That's really cool," said Ty. "Tell me about it."

Lisa said she taught three classes a week and that prospective actors could sign up for as many sessions as they like. A recital with improv skits and more were scheduled for the coming week.

"You should come," Lisa said.

Ty shook his head uncertainly. "I don't think that would really be my thing. I've never done anything like that before."

"Well that's the beauty of improv," she said. "By

definition nobody's done the same stuff before. It's always, well, improvised."

"It does sound good," said Ty, "but I'd have trouble getting there. I don't have a car."

"I can give you a ride. I'm staying in a cabin my family's renting for the summer just up the next road. My parents visit most weekends. Weekdays I'm on my own."

Lisa stopped and looked Ty up and down. "How old are you anyway?" she asked. "I've got to decide whether I'm flirting with you or not."

Ty laughed. "Good grief, are you direct or what? I'm afraid I'm younger than you think. I'm 17, just finished my junior year of high school. How old are you."

"Oh, that's too bad, I'm a freshman in college. Yeah, that's no good. You do look older. You shouldn't have told me how young you are."

Ty looked shocked.

"I'm just messing with you, Ty. Lighten up. That's what I do, shake things up, say and do the unexpected. You need to be prepared for such things. How are you ever going to be good at improv? That's why you need to come to the improv class. Will you?"

Ty studied her pretty, earnest face. "My potential as an actor's only part of it, right? You're short of students?"

"Maybe. That could have something to do with it."

Ty laughed. "Alright I'm in. I'm starting to warm to the idea anyway. Let me go grab the rest of the gear from the shed."

Soon they were back at the river and Ty had fixed

Lisa's paddle. They nosed their boats into the water and readied to push off.

"How are you getting back from the takeout?" Ty asked.

"I left my truck at the bridge and rode my bike back."

"Could you fit my canoe in your truck, too? If so, I could paddle with you and hop a ride back. Otherwise, I'd just paddle up here where it's wide and slow."

"Sure, I've got a small, old Toyota truck with ratchet straps that'll keep the canoe and kayak from tipping out the back. Let's go. I'd be happy to have you along. When I'm paddling alone sometimes guys holler and try to hit on me. With you along, I probably won't get that."

"Happy to help," Ty said, looking at her as they climbed in their boats and paddled off. "I know what you mean. When I wear a bikini top and cutoffs like you do, I get a lot of catcalls, too."

"Wise guy."

"I couldn't resist. Tell me how you got into teaching acting."

Lisa said she'd acted in high school and was a theater major at Shepherd University, which has a top theater program and hosts the famous Contemporary American Theater Festival. In high school she'd helped teach acting to elementary school kids in an after-school program. Teaching improv to teens and adults at the Art Haus was a logical next step.

"Alright, well I'm sold on your credentials," Ty said. "I'm impressed."

Ty scanned the river ahead. "Oops, we better go

single file. That narrow smooth tongue on the left between the boulders is my favorite way through here. Go ahead, I'll follow."

As Ty waited for Lisa, he marveled at the scenery. As often as he ran the river, it was different every time. The water was higher or lower, sometimes muddy, sometimes so clear that you could reach down and snatch a slider or other turtle off the bottom and set it back down.

I wish I could get out in the mornings before work, Ty thought to himself. Early morning was the best time to see wildlife, as the critters foraged and drank from the river at first light. The previous year he and Walt had seen a mother black bear and a cub directly across from the put-in where they'd just launched.

"Hey, look at that," Lisa said. "There's a new rope swing in that huge tree on the left."

"Could be trouble," Ty said.

"I don't see why, the owners aren't there. There's no poison ivy near the base."

"Yeah, you're right. You pull up first. I'll follow in behind you."

Lisa beached her kayak, clambered up the bank, and grabbed the knot handholds on the thick hemp rope and paused. The only sound was the water dripping off the bottom of the rope.

"It's a little scarier when you're up on the bank isn't it?"

"Yeah, but I'm not going to chicken out. Here goes." Lisa pulled up on the rope, kicked off from the bank, and dropped knife like into the water, arms over her head, hardly making a splash.

First to bob back to the surface was Lisa's bikini top. Lisa followed, arms folded and clamped tightly across her chest. She looked anxiously side to side, eyes wide.

Ty howled with laughter. "Let's try a little improv, in shallow water. You're a volleyball player setting up your teammate to spike it."

"Oh aren't you so clever," she said, angrily. "You'll get your payback. This was the 'trouble' you warned me about wasn't it?"

"It was just hypothetical. I'd never seen it happen. Didn't want to rush to any conclusions. Stay where you are. I'll bring you your top and climb up on the bank and keep my back turned until you tell me I can turn around."

"Okay you can turn around," Lisa said moments later, climbing back up the bank and throwing the rope back to Ty for his turn on the swing. As Ty stood gathering his nerve, one hand on the rope, Lisa gave him a sharp shove from behind.

"Yow!" Ty said, falling into the river beside the rope and landing ankle deep in the muddy river bottom. He surfaced spluttering to the sound of Lisa's laughter, his feet stuck in a muddy weed bed. "I guess I deserved that."

"That makes us even," Lisa said. "No hard feelings?"

"Nope, fair's fair."

They continued their leisurely three-mile run down to the low-water bridge, with stops to admire the scenery. At the takeout, two families were lazing above the bridge – parents in folding chairs chatting, young kids splashing in the shallows.

Ty offered the kids a ride in the canoe. He helped lift them in and handed them paddles, allowing them to spin the boat in circles for a few minutes. Afterward, Lisa and Ty loaded up the truck for the return trip.

Lisa dropped Ty at his cabin, saving him carrying the canoe uphill.

"Thanks Ty," she said. "That was fun, though I do see you've got a little rascal in you, not that that's bad. You'll be needing that edge at the improv class tomorrow."

"Okay. You're going to pick me up at six for the six-thirty class, right?"

"That's right. See you then."

Ty stood in the driveway and waved as Lisa backed out and drove away. Next he went inside, ate dinner, and fell asleep reading in bed.

The next morning he walked over to Thurston's and they returned to the flooring job. They'd finished the great room. Next up were the three bedrooms.

Thurston and Ty worked for two hours then took a break, walking outside to sit on rocks, drink coffee from the thermos, and chat.

"So Romeo," Thurston said, "how are things going with Casey? You were in full pursuit there before we took last week off."

"There are all sorts of things coming to a head," Ty said. "The good news is she came to pick me up at the airport and let me take her to dinner. The bad news is that she's still going out with Vincent and he's coming out here this weekend with her."

"That's too bad," said Thurston. "I've told you he

struck me as spoiled, showing off his new BMW. And did I tell you he almost got beaten up out here, earlier this summer?"

Ty looked surprised. "What happened?"

"Oh it was great fun to watch. I'm coming across the low-water bridge and he's crawling along the road in the bimmer, staring at this girl in the river. She's coming out of the water in a t-shirt and shorts, head back, shaking the water out of her hair, just like in a movie or something. He pulls over, never taking his eyes off her. He gets out and tries some lame line on the girl, who scowls, shakes her head and walks past him."

"Wow, what a dog. And he did this while out visiting Casey? Man, that makes me mad!"

Thurston chuckled. "That's not even the best part. Because Vincent hadn't looked around, he never saw the huge dude she was with. The guy had been up in the back of his pickup fetching chairs and a cooler with his back turned. So he sees this guy hassling his girl, jumps down, and puts his hand up to signal me to let him pass, which I'm delighted to do, having a front-row seat and all. The guy runs over to Vincent, who's got his back turned. The big dude grabs Vincent's arm, spins him around and shoves Vincent in the chest, knocks him on his butt. Vincent sees the size of the guy, scrambles to his feet, runs to his car and takes off."

"Unbelievable! And here's Casey being so kind to this cheater wannabe, while I'm being a perfect gentleman. Good grief. If only Casey could have seen that!"

CHAPTER 7

Ty was finishing his dinner dishes when he heard the beep of a car horn in the driveway. He saw Lisa waving from her truck. He jogged out and climbed in.

"I've got to admit, I'm a little nervous about this," Ty said. "I'm afraid I'll freeze up or be too timid. You've got to just let it rip, right?"

Lisa smiled. "That's it, you want to go for it with gusto. Remember, this is a small town in the doldrums of summer. There are only six students, most have no acting experience. Some are kids, some are seniors. Everybody's friendly. Plus, I'll have a couple old hands go first. And by old hands, I mean people who've been to at least one class."

"That's a relief. Thanks."

"So what else are you doing out here all by yourself for the summer? You're working construction, becoming a river rat, what else?"

Thoughts whirled in Ty's head. He couldn't tell her about the gnomes. She'd think him crazy and make him walk home. "Well, since you say I'm too young to have a chance with you, I can confess that I'm chasing a girl, Casey."

"Very gallant how you put that. Thanks for sparing my feelings. So, tell me the story of this Casey who's stealing you away."

"Unfortunately she's already stolen, by a cad, no less. His name's Vincent. It's up to me to steal her back, not that she was mine in the first place, but you get the idea."

"A cad, I like that. What did he do?"

"He pestered a mean dude's girlfriend. Had he been a step slower he might have been badly beaten."

"So how's that leave things?"

"Casey's coming up from Baltimore with Vincent this weekend and I'll have just one chance to see her." Ty explained that Casey said they could all go canoeing together but only if Ty brought a friend.

Ty paused. "I wish I could just pull Casey aside and tell her how Vincent is disrespecting her."

"So who are you going to invite as your canoeing buddy?"

"I was thinking my boss, Thurston."

"Why, does Vincent like guys? How intriguing."

"No. I mean not that I know of. What's that got to do with it?" Ty looked puzzled for a moment then his eyes went wide. "Good grief, you think I should invite a girl, hoping that Vincent will hit on her so Casey will see for herself what he's really like?"

"That's about it," Lisa said with a grin. "Except we're not going to leave it to chance."

"Oh, so you're in on this, too? You want to come

along? Oh my, I don't think I can handle that. You're too into drama, literally. You'd risk blowing everything up just to follow your outrageous script."

"Don't say 'script,' Ty, please. It would be improv. You can't have a script for just two of the four actors. And not to worry, I won't go for 'outrageous' as you say. I'd just hope that some humor and emotion would emerge."

Lisa glanced at Ty. "Oh Ty, you look very worried."

"That would never work," Ty said. "It would just be a game to you."

"Never work, huh? Do you doubt my feminine charms?"

"Good heavens, no. It's not that. Vincent won't stand a chance. You're too cunning and wicked."

Lisa bit her lip and blinked like she might cry.

"I'm sorry," Ty said, horrified. "I didn't mean to ..." His eyes narrowed. "Oh crap, you're playing me."

Lisa giggled. "It's what I do."

"Alright," Ty said wearily. "You're my best and only hope. Can you promise me that if we expose Vincent that will be it? You won't keep milking the situation for more drama, some spectacular finale?"

"Okay," Lisa said, reluctantly. "Fair enough."

"Great. We've got a deal. In return I promise I'll come to some of your classes. I'll play whatever crazy improv antics you want."

Ty sat silent, looking out the window as they crested the ridge and began the series of switchbacks that led into Warm Springs.

Lisa looked over at him. "You look a bit dazed, Ty. Snap out of it. Be resourceful and positive. You just drove your friend to Wyoming to win the love of his life. All you'll need to do for yourself is canoe and follow my lead."

By now they'd come through the outskirts of town and pulled into a parking space beside the hulking Art Haus building. Lisa turned off the ignition and looked at Ty.

"I'll be serious with you Ty. We're going to win you this girl. But I'll need your help. I may need a cue, an action, a distraction, something that makes the situation flow right and be believable."

"I would feel a little bad about this," Ty said. "I'd be tricking Casey after all."

"No, you won't be tricking Casey. You'll just be letting Vincent show his real nature. Casey's just the audience. She can choose to forgive Vincent or not. That's for her to decide."

"Alright, I'm sold," Ty said.

Lisa and Ty walked into the Art Haus together into a windowless studio with black walls. Ty was relieved there'd be nobody watching their session. Several students were already there.

"Everyone, this is Ty," Lisa said cheerily.

"Hi, Ty," the others said in unison.

"Ty this is Doug, Lou, Kelly, Diane, and Karen. Now with you joining in we'll have two groups of three and will mix up the trios over the course of the class. We'll do some stretching exercises first to help get loose and relaxed. Then we'll start."

Ty scanned his fellow students. They ranged in age from high school to retirees. Some were locals, some were vacationers. All seemed relaxed and friendly.

Lisa called on Ty, Lou, and Karen to go first. "Okay guys, Ty and Karen are gardeners working in a front yard while Lou is driving a Brinks truck with its rear door open and hundred dollar bills flying out the back. Ty and Karen, you two start snatching up and hiding the bills as fast as you can from Lou, who turns around and is very suspicious to see just one bill lying on the ground."

The group all chuckled, imagining the possibilities.

"Now remember," Lisa said, "I want to see the whole works – dialogue, teamwork, sight gags, everything. Lou, please get in your van and start driving."

A madcap skit ensued. Lou came racing around the imaginary corner, steering and disappearing offstage.

Karen ran over to the imagined road to whirl her arms, indicating the bills swirling in the wind. The two started stuffing money in their pockets and up their shirts.

"It's too much to carry," Ty said, falling to the floor in pushup position. "Let's use the wheelbarrow."

"Great idea," said Karen, dumping bills on his back and lifting Ty's feet as he walked on his hands offstage to empty the wheelbarrow.

"Let's bury some money in a hole," Karen said, and the two started mad digging motions.

Lou came running back, demanding, "Where's all the money?" Next he frisked the others who handed more loot back and forth behind Lou's back.

Shortly, Lisa yelled "cut" and gave the next group their setting. "This will be another crime caper. Doug has robbed a bank, Diane is a police officer chasing him down the street, and Kelly works at the makeup counter in a department store. Doug dashes in looking for disguises and asks Kelly for an extreme makeover while being questioned by Officer Diane.

The class did that sketch and some other exercises. Afterward they went next door to buy ice cream and sit together on the lawn.

"That was lots of fun," Ty said on the way home. "I really enjoyed that."

Lisa dropped Ty at the cabin and looked at it curiously. Ty was about to invite her in when he noticed an odd bulge in a shadow thrown by a nearby white oak.

"Thanks for the ride, Lisa," he blurted out. "I'd invite you in but the cabin's a mess. Some other time?"

"Sure," Lisa said. "I can tell your grandpa did a beautiful job building it. I'd enjoy seeing it."

After the sound of Lisa's truck was just a receding buzz on the river road, Jasper and Nate stepped out of the shadows.

"Surprise," said Jasper.

"We brought deer jerky," said Nate. "We've been getting curiouser to talk to you."

Ty grinned, ran over and scooped the two up in his arms. This was a mistake.

Like all gnomes, Jasper and Nate were stout, muscular, and quick. They reflexively pummeled Ty on the shoulders, nose, and ears until he yelped and let them drop.

"Never grab a gnome," Jasper said cheerfully. "It's instinct for us to fight if grabbed. We can't help it."

Nate giggled. "This causes trouble for gnomes, too. The morning after Gnome One was married, he appeared at assembly with a fat black eye. He'd rolled over in his sleep and given his wife, Pixie, a tight squeeze. Wee thing that she was, she still gave him a good punch, without even waking up."

"Okay, I've learned my lesson," Ty said. Hearing a rustling sound, he looked up at the tree overhead.

"Ah jeez, now comes the next hazard," he said. Talon had landed during the scuffle, and was staring intently at Nate's tote bag.

"Talon's after his jerky."

Nate tossed a piece to the bird and the three hustled inside to avoid being seen by passersby.

"So, you must tell us everything about convertibling to Wyoming with Marvin," Jasper said. "Is Marvin riding off into the sunset with Anna on the back of a horse like in the movies?"

"I don't think Marvin is riding," said Nate. "Marvin cannot ride a horse. I think he is wobbling around if trying riding because he is falling on his head."

"I don't know what's happened either," Ty said. "Let's hike to the ridge and call him."

"Oh, oh," said Nate. "Can I talk in the jabber box?"

"We'll see," Ty said as they started uphill on an overgrown logging road. "We'll need to keep the call pretty short."

The hike took thirty minutes at a quick pace. The gnomes could have done it in half the time but were still impressed at Ty's fitness. "You do well for a biggie. But you can't do this," said Nate leaping five feet straight up in the air and feigning a yawn while waiting to touch ground again.

"Show off, try this," muttered Jasper, running at and up a tree until he did a backflip, landing on his feet. "Four running steps on the tree."

Ty gaped at these acrobatics, as the gnomes chuckled.

From the top of the ridge they had a beautiful view. The other side of the river canyon was bathed in the orange light of the setting sun. A pileated woodpecker took to its distinctive swooping flight, its bright red head shining in the sun. It landed in a tree nearby and began walking up the trunk, searching for grubs.

Ty watched then pulled his phone from his pocket. "Okay, let's call Marvin. That's what we're here for after all."

The gnomes by his side, Ty dialed and Marvin answered on the third ring. "Ty, is that you?"

"Yes Marvin," Ty said eagerly. "It's great to hear your voice. Are you and Midnight alright?"

"Oh yes Ty, it is very fun and exciting. Midnight was a little sad when you left but he likes to be a cow finder and is very excited to be running all through the hills and prairie helping to look for Anna. The Internet was very right about dogs with their good sniffers. I found some cow hair on a barbed-wire fence and held it for Midnight to sniff. I was so excited, I yelled to Midnight. I said, "Go Midnight use your great cow sniffer and find us cows and Anna, too!"

"And we found our very own cow. It is a baby, called a calf. Actually, it's a boy cow, called a steer, so a steer calf, I think. It's confusing. Anyway, its back feet were stuck in mud and it was scared. It is old enough that it doesn't need milk, and I think its mother was scared away. He is very happy to be with us now. We are a good team of Anna hunters, one gnome, one calf, and one dog. Midnight is learning to herd. He goes to catch the calf, "Mudlegs," when he goes too far from us.

With Midnight and Mudlegs we have put up many flyers. We are looking still for Anna. You should not worry. We are taking down the tent poles in the daytime and are in a grove of trees so nobody can see our cowboy camp. We still have a lot of food left and are cozy in our camp, so you don't need to worry. I'm very brave even when I hear a coyote howl at night."

"Have you seen any biggies?" Jasper asked.

"We see them driving on the road in their trucks. The old ones are lazy, always driving. A few young ones, probably from the college, come walking and exploring with backpacks."

Marvin paused for a moment. "Oh, and the biggest news of all, I should have told you at the beginning. This is very exciting. One day we saw an American Indian, a Native American, religious man. He was praying on top of some high rocks. We were exploring. Mudlegs nuzzled the man as he sat praying with his eyes closed. He opened one eye, smiled, then closed that eye again. I'm showing you how he looked but you cannot see me through the phone. I will show you later."

Ty was getting exasperated. "Get on with the story, please, Marvin. Did you talk to him?"

"Yes! That was the best part. He did not seem surprised at all to see a gnome, dog, and calf team of cowboys. Maybe it's because he sees spirits and magical creatures when he has his eyes closed, so he is not surprised when he sees them with his eyes open. Or maybe he was just napping and was not surprised because he has seen gnomes before – Anna and her family! Of course he's already seen dogs and cattle before."

"Did you ask him about Anna?" Nate asked.

"Yes. I asked whether he knew a cowgirl gnome, maybe her parents, too. He was clever that man. He did not answer directly. He said I should tell him my name and where we were camping, so he would know what to tell the gnome family if he saw a family like that."

"Do you think he knew?" Ty asked.

"Yes, he had a twinkle in his eye. I told him my name and that Anna was a friend of mine and that I had come from West Virginia to look for her. I think he does know Anna and will tell her I am looking for her. I'm very excited."

"That's great news," Ty said, as Nate and Jasper started jumping up and down in excitement, making goofy faces and kissing and hugging motions.

They said goodbye, hung up, and walked back down the mountain. On their way, Nate and Jasper said they wished they could be cowboys, too, and go convertibling across the country. Ty and the gnomes parted at the turn to the cavern.

Ty was in good spirits when he returned to the cabin. Before turning in for the evening, he went out to the shed to nose around. While in Warm Springs with Lisa at the Art Haus, he had noticed rustic chairs for sale in the shop. He had seen similar ones at the gnomes' cavern and in Travis' cabin – the four chairs around the dining table. What he found in the shed bore out his hunch. Stout cherry branches, between one and three inches in diameter, were neatly stored in tall bins.

Ty asked Thurston about the wood the next day, as they drove to the next jobsite. "Thurston, do you know whether Grandpa Travis made the rustic furniture that's on permanent display in the Art Haus shop? I noticed he's got bins of cherry stock in his shed plus a lot of spade bits and tenon cutters."

Thurston said yes, Travis had made and sold quite a number of chairs, headboards, coat racks and other pieces.

"This is going to sound weird," Thurston said. "But have you ever shifted your weight in one of those chairs? It sounds new agey but you can feel them sway like the branches would have in the wind. It's a cool feeling."

Ty laughed. "Yes, it's an odd but cool feeling. Do you have any idea how they sold in the store?"

"Pretty well, I think."

"You know what, then," Ty said. "I'm going to try my hand at building some myself. What you're paying me is totally fair. But I need to earn some more money so I can go fetch my buddy and dog back from Wyoming. He may be ready to come home pretty soon and still doesn't drive."

"Good for you. Yeah, you may be able to sell some of those chairs. Meanwhile, how're things shaping up for this weekend's canoe trip with Casey?"

"Well, I have found the perfect canoeing partner. It's the girl Lisa I went canoeing with. She teaches acting and improv at the Art Haus."

"Interesting," said Thurston with a laugh. "So do you think this girl Lisa will catch Vincent's wandering eye?"

"Absolutely no doubt there. My only worry is that with her improv background she will want to take this gotcha moment to a new level and make it some epic scene. That scares the heck out of me."

"Dang, I'm sorry I'm going to miss it. I might just happen downstream in a kayak myself. You couldn't very well just shoo your boss away, right? And I might just have a knack at improv myself. I could think of a comment to throw in just to juice up the situation a bit. What do you say?"

"Yeah, that's great, someone else to sabotage my chances, just in case Lisa should surprise me by showing some restraint."

Friday he and Thurston quit early, at 3 p.m., so Ty could take his time hiking to the ridge to call Casey before she left for their cabin.

He took a deep breath and phoned at 3:45.

"Hi Ty," she said pleasantly.

"Hi Casey. It's nice to know you recognize my number. You're still coming up this weekend, right?"

"Yes, I'm in my room packing my stuff. We're going to leave after dinner, at about 7 p.m. Vincent's staying with us. So you've got Thurston lined up as your canoeing buddy?"

"No, Thurston's not coming, I'm afraid."

"Ty, we had a deal. What did I say about you not

coming alone?"

"Oh, I won't be coming alone. I'm bringing a different friend, a girl. Her name's Lisa. I've already tried her out."

"Tried her out?" Casey said, incredulous.

"Yes, we paddled together this week," Ty said, innocently, "What did you think I meant? She's a kayaker and has done lots of canoeing, too. She will be great, even if the river's up."

There was a moment of silence on Casey's end. "So, where did you meet her?"

"Down at the river. I'd carried my canoe down and she came up a moment later carrying her kayak. She was having trouble with her paddle so I helped her fix it. We got to talking and then paddled downriver together. So are you all driving up together?"

"No, I'm driving up with my parents. Vincent is driving his car. My parents won't let me drive with him on the highway. They say he's a reckless driver. My dad also thinks he's too old for me at 19. He's a holdback."

Casey explained Vincent had repeated a grade to have an extra year of sports eligibility.

"Shoot, these are other reasons you should be with me. I'm your age and a safe driver. Heck, I've proved I can drive all the way to Wyoming just fine, without being distracted by an excitable gnome and dog as passengers."

Casey laughed. "Always trying to work your charms, aren't you? But you're working them elsewhere, too, with this other gal up the holler?"

"Hey, I'll call your bluff there. You decide to go out

with me and you'll never see or hear of Lisa or any other girl again. But in the meantime, I'm pretty sure you'll like her. She's very sharp, a college theater student, and quite a presence. You'll see."

Casey said she had to get back to her packing, so they hung up and Ty walked back to the cabin. Before starting dinner, he went out to Travis' shed and picked out his old workhorse of an all-metal power drill, inserted the end of the tenon cutter in the chuck and tightened it. Then he found a stout cherry branch and cut perfectly smooth, even tenons on both ends and used a spade bit of matching size to cut recesses in two longer upright pieces.

"Just like that," he said aloud, "the start of a ladder-back chair. How cool."

Next, he walked back into the cabin and made dinner. He felt lonely without Midnight's company. I'll have to go fetch Midnight and Marvin soon, he said to himself.

Later, Ty hopped a ride into town with Thurston and bought groceries for the coming week. He also bought lunch fixings and bottled water to take on the river.

Saturday morning he was up early and had already carried the two canoes and gear down to the river by the time Lisa, Casey, and Vincent arrived.

They made their introductions and drove in two vehicles to the takeout. Lisa and Ty rode in her truck, while Casey and Vincent followed in his BMW.

Ty and Lisa rode in silence for a few minutes, with the windows down, enjoying the breeze off the river and the flickering sun and shade through the trees.

"They're right behind us," Lisa said. "Turn to look at me and let loose a big laugh and I'll do the same. We want Casey a wee bit jealous and Vincent suspecting nothing."

Ty obliged but said, "Thanks for the vote of confidence. Rather than us faking it you could have just said 'be your usual witty and charming self.'"

Lisa patted his knee. "That might be worth the risk if you'd had at least two of my improv classes. I'm that good. Meanwhile, I'm not sure your humor's quite up to it yet. And, listen, when we get on the river, just relax and react naturally to what I do."

Back at the put-in below Travis' cabin, the four donned their lifejackets, stowed the coolers and pushed off from the bank. Lisa and Ty were in one canoe. Casey and Vincent were in the other.

The initial stretch was slow and wide, the current carrying them downstream at the equivalent of a slow walking pace. But soon the river narrowed into quick-flowing rapids. Ty and Lisa paddled into the rapids first, with Ty at the helm, expertly making small adjustments to keep the canoe down the center of the channel, avoiding both rocks and running aground.

Once through, Ty pulled the canoe into slow water near the bank and looked back. To his relief, he saw that Casey, at the helm of the second canoe, had followed his line easily and confidently.

"Good work, Casey," Ty called out. "You must have run this river a lot."

Casey smiled. "Thanks."

For lunch they stopped at a large flat rock in the middle of the river, at the base of a high cliff. "Cool spot," said Vincent.

"Yeah," said Ty. "And it's got some colorful history. During the civil war, Union soldiers captured confederates hiding out in that cave at the foot of the cliff."

After lunch, Lisa spoke up. "How about we switch it up here so Casey and I share one canoe and Ty and Vincent share the other?"

Vincent and Casey looked uncertain but shrugged and agreed. Ty shot Lisa a pleading look, hoping she'd reveal what she had in mind but Lisa averted her eyes and began hauling the girls' canoe off the rock and into the river.

Ty and Vincent did the same and pulled ahead.

"So, Casey," said Lisa when the boys were out of earshot. "You know Ty is absolutely crazy about you?"

"Oh, is he? I thought maybe he'd fallen for you, an older woman and all that. He told me you're in college, and you just showed up out of the blue. How'd you meet?"

Lisa laughed. "No, Ty's a great kid but just a friend. I wouldn't date a junior in high school, two years younger than me. We met at the river Monday afternoon. I'm renting a place for the summer on the next road over from his. We met at the river, where he helped me fix my paddle. We paddled together down to the low water bridge."

Casey nodded. "That's exactly what he told me."

"Hold on, look at the two boys up there."

Casey saw Ty and Vincent stopped, drifting downriver with paddles on their knees and looking back at the girls intently.

Casey laughed. "They look stricken don't they?"

"Yes, they know we're talking about them. So why did you want to paddle with me? Was there something you wanted to say?"

"Yes, there is something I'd like to talk to you about, and I'm doing this entirely on my own. Ty would kill me if he found out."

Casey looked intrigued. "Okay, so what is it?"

Lisa took a breath. "Ty's boss Thurston told him that earlier this summer he saw Vincent hitting on a local girl whose boyfriend came very close to beating Vincent to a pulp. Ty said he'd never tell you because nobody likes a tattletale."

Casey's eyes narrowed. "Did Ty put you up to this? If so, this is the lowest thing ever and I'll never speak to him again."

"Absolutely not, like I said. You know Vincent. You know whether he's capable of this. If not, forget about it."

Casey's face clouded over. "Honestly, I don't know what to think. If I talk to you frankly will you keep it to yourself? I feel like I can trust you but I want your word."

"Absolutely."

"Okay then. Yes, Vincent is getting pushy with me, he wants more affection, and he does everything on impulse. But if he's actually scoping out and hitting on girls behind my back, that would be the last straw, that's for sure."

"Well, let's put him to the test then."

"Put him to the test? Good grief, how?"

"There's a rope swing around the next bend. Let's

stop there for a swim. We'll see what Vincent reveals about himself. Just keep an eye on him."

Casey chuckled. "What's this, a sting operation?"

"More or less." Lisa grinned. "Hey guys," she yelled, "there's a rope swing around the next bend on the right. Let's stop there for a swim."

Ty and Vincent looked at each other and nodded. "Sure," Vincent yelled.

The boys sat still in the canoe, waiting for the girls to catch up.

Vincent looked at Ty, eyes narrowed. "I know what you're trying to do. You're trying to steal Casey away from me. She mentioned she'd met a 'nice guy' and you're trying to horn in, I can tell. Casey's the first girl you see so you're after her, with your tongue hanging. You're just a hermit living alone in your little hut."

Ty laughed. "Maybe not for long," he said, with a wink. "Look around you."

"What? Are you telling me you think Lisa will move in with you? Oh my, are you kidding? She is so hot."

"No, I don't really think so. She says I'm too young for her. I'm seventeen and she's nineteen. She said she can't 'rob the cradle.'"

"It's tough to be you. I happen to be nineteen."

"Nineteen and still in high school? Did you repeat a year?"

"Not because I had to, smartass, because another year in school is getting me into a college with a better lacrosse team."

Looking past Vincent, Ty saw Lisa step out of the girls' canoe and climb the steep bank to a tall sycamore, where a fat rope hung out over the water.

Vincent turned to look, too.

"I'll go first," she yelled, pulling off her t-shirt, and shorts, revealing the bikini she'd worn when canoeing with Ty on Monday.

Ty looked on, stunned, remembering Lisa's last rope swing adventure.

Vincent was having different thoughts. "Oh my, look at that bikini. Casey would never wear a suit like that. It's too bad. She's needs to learn to loosen up."

Lisa stretched out on tiptoes, grabbed a knot in the rope high above her head, and kicked off from the bank. She sailed well out over the river, let go of the rope and, to Ty's relief, this time clamped her arms firmly across her chest before hitting the water. She surfaced, swam back to the canoes and stood, throwing back her hair.

Ty quick stole a glance at Vincent, then Casey. Vincent's eyes were locked onto Lisa with a wolfish look, scanning her up and down.

Casey watched with growing rage, then swung her paddle fiercely into the water, sending a sheet of water crashing across Vincent's face. "You pig, Vincent!"

Vincent opened his mouth to defend himself. "I was just..." But his words were lost as he was hit by another sheet of water.

Lisa quietly climbed back into the canoe with Casey, who began paddling furiously, propelling their canoe several lengths ahead of the boys. The four of them continued downriver in silence for the next few minutes, still processing what had happened.

Ty was admiring the scenery. The river ran through a narrow canyon, steep terrain on both sides. On the left were the predominant hardwoods and on the right was a dramatic stand of pines growing in a boulder field, extending from the river to the ridge, far above.

Many of the boulders were huge and squared off, the size and shape of small cars. As Ty scanned down from ridge down, he was puzzled to see a single wet rock at the water's edge. A moment later he heard a rustling sound, then saw a black shape lunge sharply upwards with vast strength and agility.

"A bear!" Ty hissed, pointing.

The others followed Ty's eyes and stared in awe at the young bear which leapt, zigzagging its way up the mountain, stopping once or twice to look back to be sure he wasn't being chased.

"Wow, what a magical moment," Lisa said. "That was so cool. Good eyes, Ty."

Thanks to that distraction, the four resumed talking back and forth as they paddled down to the takeout, the earlier tension forgotten, at least for the moment.

"I may have really done it this time," Vincent mumbled glumly. "I've never seen Casey so mad."

"How long have you been going out?"

"A long time. She's pretty straight laced, thinks my friends and me are too loud and crude. She'll even tell me she'd rather stay home reading a book than go out with me. How bad is that?"

"Well, I guess it depends on the book."

"Thanks jackass. I expect it's pretty well over with her now. The way she got so mad, there's a lot of bad feeling there. But tell me about Lisa. Is she going out with anybody?"

Ty chuckled. "You're not wasting any time are you?

You must be the resilient type."

Ty said he couldn't say how Vincent might do pursuing Lisa. He suggested that if Vincent wanted to see her, he should sign up for her improv classes at the Art Haus.

"I might just do that. No harm in trying. I'll just tell her I want to do a skit in which I'm learning how not to be a jerk of a boyfriend."

Ty laughed. "That just might work. You'll have to do right by her if she'll have anything to do with you."

"I'd do my best, really."

"If you want to get in touch with her, call the Art Haus. I imagine you really don't want Casey to see you asking Lisa for her number."

"True, she'd kill me."

Soon they arrived at the takeout, paddled to the gravel beach, and hauled the boats out of the water. It was a tight squeeze on the way back in Lisa's truck. Ty and Vincent rode in the back, leaning up against the cab and holding onto the canoes.

Vincent chuckled. "Boy, you wouldn't get away with this anywhere but out on these back country roads, riding in the back of a pickup, unsecured load, passengers without seatbelts, driving barefoot, etc. I could get used to this."

Lisa drove the group back to Travis' cabin, where they stowed the canoes and gear. Ty stayed at the cabin, while Lisa drove back down to the river, dropping Casey and Vincent next to his car. Lisa continued on home and Casey and Vincent stopped to talk.

The cabin was set back on a ledge behind a gravel

driveway, so Ty didn't have a clear view of the river road. He felt a bit guilty but nonetheless sat on the porch and strained to hear the conversation below. Once he heard raised voices but those trailed away. After it had been quiet for a bit again, he walked to the start of the steep slope and stole a glance. Vincent was turning his car around and driving toward the interstate, while Casey walked back to the Bakers' cabin.

Ty was tempted to rush down to talk to Casey but sensed it was too soon. That night he slept fitfully but was up early, showered, and cooking breakfast when he heard a knock at the door, opened it and found Casey looking tired, shoulders slumped, her hands thrust in the pockets of her sweatshirt.

"Look what the cat dragged in," Ty said cheerfully.

"You know just what to say," she said, mockingly. "Actually, you look pretty tired yourself."

"Do you drink coffee? I just made a pot. Can I pour you a cup?"

"That would be great," she said, looking around the cabin. "This place is really cool. It looks like all the furnishings are handmade. Wow, he's got maps, star chart, books, all kinds of neat stuff."

Ty ushered Casey to a seat and sat across from her, handing her a steaming mug of coffee and pouring another for himself.

"Look, I'm really sorry for what you've been through. Do you want to talk about it?"

"No, not yet, I think. Vincent and I broke up. That's about all I want to say about it now. Otherwise, the trip was really fun. Seeing the bear bounding up the mountain was amazing and your friend Lisa's quite a character."

Casey looked up at Ty with a searching look. "You're not in cahoots are you?"

"No," Ty said. "In fact I'm dying to know what she said to you."

"She told me the story Thurston told you and said I should keep an eye on Vincent. You know what happened after that."

"She shouldn't have done that," Ty said, quietly. "I shouldn't have told her that story. I never thought she'd just blurt that out to you. She's an actor, though, makes it her business to wring all the drama out of everything. I only confided in her because she's the only person other than you and Thurston I talk to out here, plus of course, the gnomies and they've got their own issues."

Casey nodded and raised her head. "Alright, enough about that. Can you think of something fun we could do today? Some sort of adventure that will keep me from feeling foolish and sorry for myself?"

Ty gazed out the window for a few moments then turned. "I've got it. Let's go visit the Abandoned Pennsylvania Turnpike. Can you borrow your parents' car for the afternoon?"

"Sure, they said they plan to just hang out around the cabin, reading and going for a walk. Tell me about the Abandoned Pennsylvania Turnpike."

"I can tell you more than you want to know," Ty said. He explained that the abandoned turnpike was a 13-mile stretch of highway used during the 1950s and 1960s. It had been a mistake from the start. The turnpike was two lanes wide in each direction approaching the long Sideling Hill Tunnel and Rays Hill Tunnel. But the two tunnels were only one lane wide in each direction. This was okay at first but, as traffic increased, backups stretched for miles as two lanes merged into one.

Eventually, the Pennsylvania Turnpike Commission was forced to build a bypass over the summit. That left the tunnels and road abandoned.

"Now it's like a modern ghost town," Ty said. "There are weeds growing up through the cracked pavement and you walk or ride a bike through the dark tunnels." Ty said the tunnels were spooky from water dripping overhead and because one of the tunnels was slightly curved and long enough that one can't see light at the either end of tunnel when standing in the middle.

Another great selling point was the thick bushes of delicious wild blackberries and wineberries that line the road in early summer.

"Sure," said Casey. "That sounds like fun. I'm game. I'll go back by my parents' cabin, put on my hiking boots, and get some bottled water. Do you want to stop by in about half an hour and head out from there?"

"Perfect. I'll be there.

CHAPTER 8

Ty packed a daypack with a few supplies – a canteen full of water, several granola bars, sunblock, a hat, cellphone, and powerful LED headlamps for Casey and himself. He straightened up the cabin and jogged over to the Bakers.

As he walked up the driveway, Tim Baker came down the front steps to greet him. "Great to see you again, Ty. We're heading back to Baltimore this evening after dinner. If Casey wants to, you two can eat in town on your own. Just please be back by about 8 p.m. We don't want to leave too late. I need to be at work first thing in the morning."

"We'll be back on time. Thank you, sir."

The door opened and Casey came walking down the stairs, a string bag on her back. The two climbed in the Bakers' Subaru and Casey drove out the river road, over the mountain, through town, and out to the interstate.

As they turned onto the highway following signs to

Breezewood, Pennsylvania, Casey told Ty she'd seldom been west on 70. "Nor had I," Ty said, "but I made up for it with my trip to Wyoming. I wish you could have come with me. You'd have loved it."

"I think so. I'm also eager to hear how Marvin's doing looking for Anna. Can we call him tonight?"

"Sure, let's call him from Warm Springs before dinner."

Breezewood is a thicket of gas stations and fast food joints. "It doesn't look promising, I know," Ty said. "How about we just roll in here and get subs for lunch, then stop for a picnic after we've walked a bit?"

Casey nodded. "Sure, that sounds good."

Ten minutes later they pulled into a small gravel parking lot at the foot of a hill. Leading up was a narrow path lined by knee-high grass. At the top, they came to a concrete jersey wall that marked the western end of the abandoned turnpike. Beyond the barriers were just weeds and crumbling blacktop. But in the other direction was a gently curving stretch of old highway, two lanes in each direction and a grassy median.

There was forest on both sides and thriving blackberry bushes working their way from the woods across the shoulder toward the road.

Casey and Ty stepped out on the blacktop and began walking east. Within minutes they'd forgotten the noise and blight of Breezewood and were enjoying a deserted stretch of road, accompanied only by birds swooping down to feed on the berries. The only people they met were a man and his teenage son on a cross-country bike trip, having left their home in New

Jersey just three days before.

They had stopped for a rest and Ty asked them about their trip. "What's been the highlight so far?"

"Oh definitely seeing a mountain lion as we were pitching our tent at dusk last night. That was just 15 miles back, the other side of these two old tunnels."

"Wow, you're lucky. Mountain lions are supposed to be so shy and seldom seen."

Casey and Ty waved and walked on, soon coming to the first tunnel. It definitely looked spooky without lights or other people. They stepped cautiously into the tunnel entrance, picking their way around puddles of standing water. More water dripped slowly from the cracked ceiling.

Ty reached into his bag and produced two headlights. "Here, take one of these and pull it over your head. Push the black button on top to turn it on. Take my hand. I'll go ahead and you can follow my steps. If I step in a puddle, stop so I can direct you around it without you getting your shoes soaked, too."

"Wow it's so cool in here," Casey said. "It's natural air conditioning, at least ten degrees cooler inside than out."

They walked cautiously through the tunnel for at least ten minutes, the only sound being water dripping and their voices echoing off the walls.

As they exited the tunnel, they hopped onto a concrete retaining wall and sat in the shade, while their eyes adjusted to the light.

Ty put his arm around Casey's shoulder but she brushed it off. "Please Ty, it's too soon."

She turned to face him and looked at him intently.

"Have you ever been in love?"

"You mean before now?"

Casey shook her head. "Be serious."

"I am serious," Ty insisted.

"Answer the question."

"Honestly, no. I've dated a couple of girls, never for very long, and nothing more than a mild crush. So, no, I've never been in love."

"But here you are telling me you love me."

"Yes."

"That's crazy. Teenagers don't fall in love. They think they do. There's lots of drama maybe. They break up, that's about it. You know the odds. Do you know any couples at your school who you think might really stay together?"

"I don't care about the odds. I don't care about other couples. If you and I are right for each other, we want to know that, right?"

Ty stopped and looked at her. "I don't want to be like my dad and his buddies at the bar, full of regret. Failure isn't what makes you miserable. It's what you never try."

"Alright, I'll grant you that. But I tried going out with Vincent and look where that got me, feeling like a fool."

"Enough with the self-pity. We need to snap you out of this." Ty took a step back then reached out his arm and tapped her on the shoulder. "You're it."

"What?"

"I said 'you're it.' C'mon you know how to play the game. Everybody does. You're just stalling because you know you can't catch me."

133

Casey's eyes narrowed. "It'd be too easy, not even worth it."

Ty tapped her again, this time on the top of her head.

"Oh, you are really asking for it," Casey said sternly.

Ty started to reach for her again but she lunged at him. He leapt back, just dodging the swipe of her hand.

"Yow," he said, turning and sprinting down the cracked road. He slowed slightly so he could look back without getting his feet tangled. In a flash, Casey caught him and gave his shoulder a hard shove, enough that he staggered sideways, almost fell, then recovered and stood panting, hands on his knees.

Casey stopped a good distance away, gasping for breath, too.

"I underestimated you," Ty said. "I thought you softball players could only run as far as the next base. Alright, I'm it. I'll give you a head start. Ready, go!"

Casey raced off with Ty in pursuit. "Not much of a head start," she muttered.

Ty caught Casey a few yards later, grabbed her by the waist and lifted her in the air, both of them laughing and struggling to catch their breath. Ty let go of her and she turned to face him.

"Thanks Ty. You really are helping me feel better. Thanks."

They retrieved their packs and walked back to the car, stopping often to eat berries.

Ty looked up and down the old road. "Crazy isn't this, the way you feel lost in time on this hike. I keep looking back out of force of habit, thinking it's not safe to be walking down the middle of a highway."

Casey nodded. "Yes and all that standing water in the tunnels, the equipment rooms with the steps rusted through. It's like a ghost town."

"You know in fact this abandoned turnpike was used in the movie version of *The Road*, a post-apocalypse book."

"Oh, sure, Cormac McCarthy?"

"That's the one. Nothing's sexy like a smart, well-read woman."

Casey laughed. "That's what they all say. No, in fact, hardly anybody says that. One point for Ty."

"How many points does a guy need for boyfriend status?"

Casey sighed and looked exasperated. "Be patient Ty, please. I'm flattered but who breaks up with a guy one day and starts dating another guy the next? Will you promise me you'll give me some time?"

Ty took a deep breath. "Yes. It won't be easy but yes, I will."

He walked a few steps in silence. "Will the signal be subtle, if it comes? I would hate to miss it."

Casey shook her head and chuckled. "No you'll know if and when the time comes. I'll promise you that."

"That's a relief. I mean what if you gave me a wink but I had speck of dirt in my eye and missed it?"

Casey gave him playful shove. "Oh shut up already."

The two returned to the car and drove back to Warm Springs, where they walked to the park in the center of town. Ty said he, his dad, and his granddad would drive in on Saturday afternoons to hear concerts in the park.

Casey said her family used to do that, too, and suggested that their families ought to come into town together for a concert and dinner some time.

Ty agreed, delighted to hear Casey suggesting long-term plans that included him.

"How about we walk down to the barbecue place for dinner?" Ty asked. "It's a favorite of the gnomies but a bit stressful eating there with them. There's that difficult matter of smuggling food out to them and making sure they behave."

Casey laughed. "Sure, I love that place."

They walked slowly to the restaurant, took a seat and soon were enjoying hearty plates of pulled pork sandwiches, beans, and collard greens.

"We get a cell signal here in town. Should we call Marvin from here?" Casey asked.

"How about we do that from the Panorama lookout? It will be near sundown, when the view is so awesome up there."

Casey agreed and after dinner they drove to the lookout at the top of the ridge and backed into a space. That way they could open the hatchback of the Subaru and sit facing the Potomac River valley, their legs dangling over the rear bumper.

"Ready to make the call?" Ty asked. Casey nodded, eager to hear Marvin's latest news.

Marvin answered on the first ring.

"Ty is that you? I am so excited to be hearing you, or I will be when I know it's you."

Ty laughed. "Yes, of course it's me. It's great to hear your voice. Do you have any news?"

"Only the most fabulous news there could be. I found Anna! She saw one of my notes, the kind we put in the plastic to keep out the rain. She came looking for me. She was almost finding our camp by nightfall and stopped to camp herself. Midnight and I went out and found her first. It was very exciting. I will tell you all about it later."

"That's great news!" Ty said.

"Yay!" whooped Casey.

"Who is that 'yay' person?" said Marvin. "Is that Casey?"

"Yes," Ty said. "It's wonderful that she's here. I'm crazy about her like you are for Anna and she doesn't have her old boyfriend. I'm not her new boyfriend but I've let her know I'm available. Ow. Sorry, Casey just punched me."

"Not hard like a gnome punch, I hope" said Marvin, alarmed.

"No, not that hard," Ty said. "Please don't teach her any gnome punches either. So where is Anna now?"

"She's right here, Ty. The best thing is that she wants to come back to the gnome cavern. She says she likes being a topsider but wants to come back with me to visit her old gnomies. Then she will decide whether she wants to stay in West Virginia or go back to Wyoming. I will go wherever she wants to go and will be happy."

Marvin said that when they arrive in West Virginia, Anna wants to meet Ty and thank him for driving Marvin to Wyoming.

"Of course, of course, Marvin. May I speak to her?"

"Yes, on the telephone. You will find she is like the

Internet when it comes to cows. She knows everything. For instance, she knows that cows are like big compasses. When they lie down they are always aimed north and south. I think one end is north and the other is south, not always the same end. This is cow science and she knows things like that. Isn't that interesting?"

"Yes, that's great. Today I was just telling Casey how great it is that she is so smart but probably not about cow science. So put Anna on, please."

"Hi Ty," said a soft voice after a moment's pause.

"Hi Anna, that's wonderful news that you will be coming home. Marvin has told us so much about you and we had a wonderful trip together coming out to search for you." Ty said he was sorry he couldn't stay to help him look for her but knew Marvin and Midnight would do a great job searching.

"Yes, I have missed Marvin and the other gnomies very much. Young gnomes like to have lot of friends around so we can have our jokes, pranks, school, businesses, and adventures together. I am looking forward to meeting you and seeing all my old friends."

Ty assured Anna that he and Casey were very eager to meet her, too, and wanted to hear all about her life in Wyoming and how Marvin and Midnight found her. He said he worried, though, about the cellphone running out of battery and asked to speak to Marvin again.

"Marvin, very quickly now, tell me how you plan to come back home. Do you need me to come get you?"

"No, this is great news. Anna has an Indian friend whose nephew drives a truck. She says some biggie

Indians believe in spirits and know all about gnomes."

"Wow, how cool, but tell me all that later. Just tell me now how you're getting home, okay?"

"Yes, yes," Marvin said, reluctantly. "The nephew he is truck driving to Roanoke, Virginia. He's driving beef in a refrigerated trailer that has a sleeper cab." Marvin said he and Anna would sleep in the truck while the nephew slept in the hotel. The nephew will come east on Interstate 70, then drop them at the bottom of Ty's road Friday evening at sundown, before driving back to the highway and on to Roanoke.

"That's wonderful, door to door service. Okay, see you soon and use the phone if you have any trouble. If not, call when you're close to home. Have a safe trip!"

After saying goodbye to Marvin, Ty turned to Casey. "Wow, that all worked out so well, I almost can't believe it."

"There's plenty about this situation I wouldn't believe if we weren't in the thick of it, that's for sure."

They sat together on the tailgate and watched the sun go down.

Ty pointed to the road to his left. "I love the view there, right over the road as you wind down the switchbacks to Little Falls. Those tiers of mountains seem to stretch on forever, from blue to ever lighter shades of blue and gray. It's really this view I think of when I hear 'Blue Ridge Mountains.'"

Casey turned. "That reminds me. I read that Bill Danoff, the guy who wrote 'Country Roads' was travelling in Ireland, visiting one of the country's most famous pubs for live music. He was there listening when someone in the audience recognized him and asked him to play. And, with the first notes of 'Country Roads,' the whole audience sang along and knew all the words."

Ty laughed. "It's true. You can't say the words 'Blue Ridge Mountains' without the song starting to play in your head.

Ty looked out again over the valley, triggering a memory. "Recently I read something about this lookout that I'd never noticed. From here you can see all the historic modes of transportation west – the river, the old toll roads, the C&O Canal, the railroad, and the interstate, all in this narrow stretch."

Casey and Ty climbed back into the Subaru and drove back to the Bakers' cabin.

"Do you think you can come out here again next weekend?" Ty asked. "You'd be able to see Marvin, Anna, and Midnight and hear about their adventures."

"I'm not sure," Casey said. "I'd love to do that but my parents are heading off to a college reunion of my mom's that weekend and I don't know whether they'd let me take the other car and come out by myself. I've never asked to do that."

"You're a good student and have stayed out of trouble, right? And if you can make it, I'll promise to be a perfect gentleman. Honest."

"You mean, you'll bow, you'll pull out my chair for me, and throw your overcoat in a puddle so I don't dirty my shoes?"

Ty laughed. "I most solemnly do. And it's a good thing you asked. I normally wouldn't have my overcoat with me in the summer in West Virginia."

The Bakers came down the stairs and met them in

the driveway. "Hi guys, did you have a nice daytrip?" Tim asked.

Ty and Casey told them where they'd been and asked about the following weekend. "Dad, Ty's friend he drove to Wyoming is coming back next week with Ty's dog Midnight and a girl the guy grew up with before she took up ranching. Do you think I could come out here on my own? Ty's already told me what a gentleman he promises to be, right down to bowing, pulling out my chair for me, and so forth."

Tim chuckled. "Well done, Ty." Turning to Casey he added, "We'll see. Your mother and I will have to talk about this."

Ty returned to the cabin, happy about his day with Casey. He sat out on the front porch and tried to pick out some songs on his harmonica. He taught himself a tune that he had been struggling with, and had played it through cleanly several times, before he saw the Bakers' Subaru drive out the river road on the way home.

The next morning he walked over to Thurston's place and met him in the driveway as usual. Thurston smiled and handed Ty a travel mug of coffee. "Who says your job doesn't come with benefits?"

"These are the best benefits I've ever had. So what kind of fun do you have lined up for us today?"

Thurston said Ty would be happy with the latest gig. "At least until Wednesday we've got trim work. We've got window trim for 13 windows. We've got door trim for four doors. We've got doors to install in two clothes' closets and one linen closet. And, we've got floor trim to install throughout the house. And, like the house we did a few weeks ago, this one is new construction and air conditioned."

"That's awesome."

They worked efficiently that day. First Thurston made all the miter cuts for the window trim, and had Ty install it using a pneumatic nailer. After lunch, though, Ty had his chance to make the cuts, measuring carefully so all the trim had flush, tight joints.

Thurston complimented him on his work. "I thought this would be a good job for you to start on, because it's all cheap knotty pine and we wouldn't be out of pocket much for waste. But you did great. I'd trust you even with pricey hardwoods."

At noon they walked down to the river to eat lunch while enjoying the view. "You've got a nice life out here, Thurston," Ty said. "I envy you."

"How about you kid? What's your fall going to be like when you're back in school?"

"Well, it will be my senior year. I'll be applying to colleges and all that. But above all I hope that I'll be going out with Casey. I feel really relaxed and happy with her. I've never found a girl so easy and fun to talk to."

"Enjoy it while you can."

"Ah, c'mon, people in relationships always bellyache."

"No, you're right. You've heard Shelley and me yelling at each other. It's all good natured. We let off some steam but we wouldn't know what to do with ourselves if we were apart. Of course, we'd never admit that to each other."

"That's good to hear. Seeing my parents break up, I didn't have the best role models growing up."

"Speaking of that, how's your dad doing? Still exercising and drying out?"

Ty smiled. "You know, Thurston, I think he really is. He might just succeed. I'm pulling for him. He always did everything he could for me. He just wasn't good at taking care of himself."

Ty paused nodded up the mountain at the home they were helping finish. "What do you know about the owners?"

"Well, I've met them. I know the type. They're stressed at home and like the idea of a getaway but probably won't make much use of the place. They seem the kind that can't relax, the type who'll mind having to make their own coffee rather than hit the Starbucks drive thru."

"Well, what do you think of the Bakers?"

"I like them. I really do. They appreciate the slower pace out here. They hike, they paddle, they know their wildlife, plants, and fossils. They don't talk down to locals like me. In fact, Tim and his wife have strolled by with a six pack once or twice to sit out on the deck with my wife and me. Good folks."

Ty and Thurston worked steadily on the house through the week. Wednesday evening Ty hiked up the mountain to the turn onto the path that led to the gnomes' cavern. He'd come prepared with a folded sheet of paper and a felt tip marker.

Once he got to the point where the trail was unfamiliar he figured he'd reached the spot where the gnomes had put the hoods over their heads before leading them into the cavern. He stopped there, laid the sheet of paper on a flat rock and kneeled to write "Marvin returning Friday. Please stop by."

He then looked at the sky, nodding approvingly that it was completely clear of clouds. He then tore a small hole in the note and hung it on a branch at about waist height on a biggie, eye level for a gnome.

He then continued up the mountain to get a cell signal and see if he had any missed calls from Casey. Sadly there were none. "I miss you," he texted and walked slowly down the mountain, allowing time for a reply. His phone chirped. "Miss you, too. Please call tomorrow. With girlfriends at dinner."

Ty grinned. "Great, will call then," he texted back.

Thursday after work, Ty scrambled quickly up to the ridge, wanting to call Casey and be back at the cabin before the gnomes arrived. "Hi, are you coming up this weekend?" he blurted out when she answered.

"You get straight to the point don't you? The answer is yes, my parents say I can go."

"That's wonderful," Ty said.

Back at the cabin, Ty had barely wolfed down his supper when he heard muffled voices in the woods.

He looked out and saw three gnomes, Gnome One, Jasper, and Nate, all scurrying downhill and darting from behind one tree to the next.

"Gnome One, you're getting a little thick around the middle, you'd better look for bigger trees," Jasper hissed.

"That's bollocks, you impudent twit," said Gnome One. "I'm sleek and fast like a stallion."

"Exactly what I was thinking to myself," said Nate.

"A most majestic sight you are as always."

Jasper groaned. "Oh Nate, you're sucking up. You're just trying to get on his good side in case there's a spot of driving to be done during our trip to town tomorrow."

By this time, the three gnomes had climbed the steps to Ty's cabin and stood peeking in when Ty answered the door. Ty solemnly shook hands with them. "I'd give you each a hug but I took a sound beating last time I tried that. Come on in."

Ty told his short friends everything about the trip to Wyoming. Some of the stories so inspired Jasper that he acted them out. Most impressive was his recreation of McCullough's leap. For this, he bounded up a porch post onto the roof and took a running leap over the edge, making the mad motions of a crazed horseman, as he fell to the ground.

Nate was a bit jealous but had a dramatic role of his own to play, that of Marvin pulling off a huge cattle drive and courting Anna with song and dance.

Ty asked about the gnomes' plan for their trip to town Friday night. Gnome One said it would be the usual run. They'd stop to see Mrs. Gallagher, collect their checks, and deposit their packages.

Ty smiled. "I've got good news for you. After taking a few weeks off, Thurston plans to go to Big Mike's for poker tomorrow. You know what that means, hitching a ride and not having to ride bikes."

This was very welcome news to the gnomes, who said they looked forward to hopping aboard Thurston's truck. Ty told them the details of the other good news he'd written about in his note – that

Marvin would be arriving Friday with Anna.

"And there's another great thing," Ty said. "Casey's coming up tomorrow, too, so we'll have an especially fun celebration."

CHAPTER 9

Friday Ty had trouble focusing at work. He was distracted by thoughts of the eventful evening ahead. Fortunately he and Thurston were painting trim that day. Painting is perfect for daydreaming. Once they'd run painters' tape tight against the edges of the boards, it was just a matter of drawing the paint along in smooth, easy strokes.

When they quit for the day, Ty asked Thurston about the poker game that evening. "Are you going into Little Falls this evening to relieve Big Mike and the others of some of their extra money?"

"Yes, I think I will. The boys have been teasing me for missing the game a few weeks in a row, telling me how I've been lucky and am scared to play with them again. So, I better go set 'em straight."

"Do you mind if I hitch a ride into town with you?"

"Sure, but I think you'd better stay out of the game. Can't have your dad up here thinking I've helped turn you into a gambler."

Ty laughed. "No I wouldn't want to do that. I'd like to take some photos beside the tracks and the old viaduct, maybe shoot a freight train or two coming through with the sun behind them. I'll make my way back on my own"

Thurston nodded. "Sounds good but it's a long walk back. If I see you walking, I'll stop and pick you up."

Ty was telling the truth. He did like train photos, enough even to go online from home and search for other railfans' photos of rare trains sighted on the CSX Line along the river.

Ty didn't volunteer that on this particular evening he had other adventures in mind, too. First he'd try to join the gnomes in visiting Mrs. Gallagher, mailing the new gnome miniatures, and seeing if he could meet and hop the truck bringing Marvin, Anna, and Midnight home.

Ty ate a dinner and jogged over to Thurston's to be sure he didn't keep him waiting. He walked up the driveway to find Shelley and Thurston talking on the front porch.

"Okay, if I win again, I'll take you to the best restaurant in Warm Springs," Thurston was saying. "And if I lose I'll cook you dinner for the whole week. Deal?"

Shelley nodded and turned at the sound of Ty approaching. "Haven't you had enough time hanging around with my fool husband for a day? You must be getting soft in the head like him."

"Not at all, he's the smart one in our crew. I'm trying to catch up with him." Ty waved, climbed into the pickup, and stole a glance in the back and saw three large lumps under the tarp in the back and heard some animated whispering. Just like last time, he thought to himself.

"Let's get going," Ty said loudly, to drown out the gnomes. "It'll be dark soon."

Thurston drove the six miles to town and parked at Big Mike's house. From there Ty picked his way through the woods down to the 1910 viaduct and took a few shots of its beautiful stonework against the river and sky.

Minutes later Ty was happy to hear the rumble and whistle of a CSX freight train coming east through the river valley. He stepped down into the woods, aimed his camera up the embankment and took several shots of the blue and gold locomotive against the red and orange hues of the setting sun.

Meanwhile, the gnomes remained in town, racing house to house from Big Mike's to Mrs. Gallagher's. The gnomes found it remarkably easy to go unnoticed at an hour when most people were indoors, the only sign of life being the flickering light of their TV sets.

"Ah, my little princes," said Mrs. Gallagher, opening the door at their knock.

"At your service me lady," said Gnome One, bowing graciously.

Soon the group was settled as usual, drinking tea around the breakfast table and enjoying fresh-baked sugar cookies.

Mrs. Gallagher asked of their latest news and why Marvin had not come along on their usual post office run.

"Ah, those two tales are connected," said Gnome

One happily, telling her that Marvin had gone courting and was bringing back a long lost girlfriend, all the way from Wyoming.

"Wyoming, my goodness. In the old days around here you were considered high falutin' if you were so picky as to scout for a spouse a town or two away from home. And Marvin went clear out to Wyoming. That's true love."

Mrs. Gallagher glanced out the window. "I didn't see you stashing your lovely pink bikes this time. Did you get a ride with Thurston?"

Gnome One nodded and told her Thurston was at Big Mike's playing poker.

"We should play a bit of poker ourselves, after you've dropped your parcels and collected your checks from the mailbox," said Mrs. Gallagher. She also reminded them they should load into Thurston's truck the lights and wind generator kit they'd ordered to light the expanded workshop and power a second laptop in the cavern.

When Ty arrived at Mrs. Gallagher's, the gnomes were done with their chores and happily trading taunts and insults while playing poker using matches for chips.

As Ty took a seat to watch, he received a text message from Marvin. "Running late. Will arrive about 10 p.m. Our driver friend taught me how to make texts. Did you get this?"

Ty laughed. "Who says you can't teach an old gnome new tricks? Marvin sent me a text message. He says he'll be here at 10 p.m."

Gnome One nodded, looking impressed. "See,

there's nothing you can't teach a gnome."

Ty shook his head. "Except maybe hygiene, not fighting, not biting, not taking crazy risks, not showing off, not playing pranks..."

Gnome One shot Ty an approving look. "It seems biggies can be taught, too. Ty here is learning to make insults. Pretty basic stuff but a decent start."

Nate dealt the cards but Jasper didn't pick his up.

"I'm getting a bit bored," Jasper said. "I want to go give Thurston some help with his poker playing and see if we can get Big Mike all red in the face again. That was so much fun last time."

The others looked at each other and shrugged. They told Jasper they wanted to play a few more hands and would then come out and join him. Ty sat in for Jasper and the poker game continued.

Jasper walked out to the shed and picked up the cardboard, marker, and the life-size "J2" gnome dummy they'd used to torment Big Mike earlier. As before, Jasper crouched low and ran to Big Mike's house, taking up position in the window opposite Thurston, where he could see Big Mike's cards.

He noticed a large pile of chips in front of Big Mike and Thurston looking a bit pale.

Poor Thurston, thought Jasper, he's good at many things but poker not so much.

With the next hand, Jasper saw Big Mike betting heavily and Thurston looking like he might throw in his cards. Jasper quickly wrote "two aces" on the cardboard and held it up in the window.

Jasper could see Thurston revive. He took a breath to settle himself, raised the stakes, and won back a good half of the chips Big Mike had in front of him.

Much the same happened two hands later. Jasper held up his cardboard, Thurston's eyes went wide, and Thurston kept betting and won the hand.

Big Mike raised his hand to signal a break, drew his cellphone from his pocket, and walked into another room talking.

Meanwhile, Jasper looked over to the main road where he could see two men talking in front of the convenience store. Their voice carried in the calm evening air.

"You know," said the first man. "I didn't even need to go deer hunting once last year. Just driving from one job to another, twice I came upon somebody who'd just hit a deer. When I see that I always do three things. First I ask, 'Are you okay?' Second I ask, 'Can I make a call for you?' Third I ask 'Do you want that deer?'"

Drawn in by this, Jasper chuckled, as did the other man in the conversation.

"Yeah, they never want the deer. So, all I do is throw the deer in the back of the truck and go to the Sherriff's Department to fill in a form, else it's poaching. Then I take it to my buddy's butcher's shop and he gives me the cuts I want and keeps half the meat for himself. That saves me the trouble. Plus, I don't even have room for more in the freezer."

These were the last words Jasper heard before seeing a heavy blanket fall over him, blanking out the light. Terrified, he tried scrambling his way free but next felt Big Mike crush him to the ground. As Jasper gasped for breath, Big Mike gathered him up in an iron grip and started carrying him to the house.

"You got yourself in a whole heap of trouble, you little punk," Big Mike said, gasping for breath himself. "I'll get you in the light and see who you are. You thought I wouldn't remember from last time, suspicious as I was?"

Jasper felt Big Mike start up the steps to the front door. He struggled furiously to wriggle out of Big Mike's arms, got one arm of his own free and started flailing to bash his way free."

Big Mike grunted. "You're a strong little fella, I'll give you that," he said, shoving the door open with his shoulder, lowering Jasper to the floor, and pressed his knee in the middle of the squirming bundle to hold his prisoner in place.

Carefully he pulled back the blanket to reveal Jasper's face bright red, with an expression of pure fury. Big Mike was too big to be beaten for grabbing a gnome, as happened to Ty.

No, Big Mike was more than even a well-muscled gnome like Jasper could handle.

"Thurston, what the heck is this?" Big Mike demanded, stunned at the sight of his captive.

Thurston and the other poker players leaned in to look. "What are you, an elf?" asked Big Mike.

"I'm a gnome for goodness sakes," Jasper said, his voice shaking in rage. "You can stop gaping, you mouth-breathing numbskulls."

Big Mike turned to Thurston. "You've got a lot of explaining to do. Who is this guy?"

Thurston stood wide eyed. "I honestly have no idea."

"You mean you and him weren't in cahoots with this card cheating?"

"No. I'd see a sign come up showing me what cards you had. I knew my wife was going to be sore at me losing, so I bet on what the sign showed being your hand. I only wanted to win back what I lost. Who this guy is and why he wanted to help me, I have no idea. I'm sorry Big Mike."

Big Mike turned to face Thurston with a sly grin. "I'll forgive you your poker losses," he said breezily. "You've given me something much better. Boys, we are going to make us some big time money off this here character – elf, gnome, whatever he is."

"We're going to have us an old-fashioned circus freak show like used to come through town in the old days. This time it won't be a bearded lady or the world's fattest man on display, it's going to be the world's first live gnome show. And people are going to pay us big money to see him."

Big Mike turned to the gnome. "What's your name there little fella?"

The gnome stared sullenly, barely holding back tears of frustration. "It's Jasper," he said softly.

"Well Jasper, it's a pleasure to meet you. We're going to get along fine."

"If it's money you want, I've got some friends with money. We could probably buy you a used truck or something. How about that?"

"Please, Jasper, I already have two used trucks, both running fine. You'd have to do much better than that. No, I've made up my mind. I'll treat you fine and let you go after I've made a good bundle. Then you can go stand in a garden or something." Big Mike chuckled and nudged Jasper with his elbow.

Jasper stared into space then suddenly leapt to his feet and launched himself shoulder first at the window. One pane shattered but the wood mullions held, causing Jasper to bounce back in the room and land in a heap.

Big Mike leapt to his side, pinned Jasper to the floor, then turned to the nearest poker player. "Jimmy, go out to the shed and get me that nylon rope hanging on the back of the door."

Once Big Mike had Jasper firmly hogtied on the floor, he scooted a few feet away, pulled his phone from his pocket, and called an old friend of his, Johnny Barnes at the *Warm Springs News*

"Hey Johnny, can you get over here and bring your camera? You'll think I'm crazy, but I'd like you to take a picture of a gnome I've captured." Big Mike and Johnny had the expected conversation, the words "absurd" and "ridiculous" on one side and patient explanations on the other.

Big Mike finally won the argument. "Listen, Johnny we're going round in circles. I've told you my poker buddies can confirm what I've said. But you won't talk to them. You think it's a hoax. Okay, well come take a picture of this 'hoax' and write a story about the big fuss this country yokel made thinking he'd caught a gnome. It's still a good story right?"

"Alright," the reporter said, reluctantly. "I'll be out there soon. It's only because we go all the way back to grade school that I'll do this for you."

Back at Mrs. Gallagher's the poker party was

winding down. As they put away the cards, Gnome One said he was getting worried about Jasper. The others looked at each other in concern, then scrambled to start searching for him.

Ty went to the window facing Big Mike's house. Even from a distance, it was clear something troubling was up. He saw Big Mike lean a ladder against his house and clamber up it carrying a half sheet of plywood. He placed it over a bedroom window and hammered it in place. Next he climbed down and returned with pieces of 2x4 lumber, which he carried up the ladder one by one and screwed in place on top of the plywood.

Ty beckoned to the gnomes and Mrs. Gallagher to come watch. They all looked dismayed seeing the boards going up and hearing the steady whine of Big Mike's drill driver.

Gnome One shook his head. "We've got us a gnome code 202, abduction/hostage situation. Ty, can you help us out? Go down to the convenience store and pull an empty beer can out of the trash barrel and start staggering along the road. Then like a drunk yell out 'What song do you all want to hear?' Yell it a couple times. That will be our signal to Jasper."

Ty looked a bit puzzled at this request but did as he was told. On his second try belting out the question, he heard the gnomes, and a couple locals, yell "Free Bird!"

Ty scampered back to Mrs. Gallagher's. "Brilliant Lynyrd Skynyrd reference. So Gnome One, the other voices I heard, are they biggies who will help with the rescue?"

"Nope just Skynyrd fans and who isn't one really?" Gnome One added that there was nothing more to be done tonight. Thurston had told Shelley he'd be home by 10 p.m. and as Big Mike was back indoors, the coast was clear for hightailing it back to Thurston's truck.

"I'll run on up the road toward home," Ty said, explaining that Thurston had said he'd give Ty a lift if he saw him walking on the road.

Ty walked ahead of the others and was soothed by the dark and quiet road. The sky was completely clear, studded with stars.

While still close to town he called Casey. "Ty I'm driving," she said, "let me call you in a minute from Clear Spring. I'm just coming up to the exit."

Ty was excited. This meant Casey was only 20 miles away. Moments later she called back. "I can't wait to see you," Ty said, then also told her the bad news of Jasper's capture.

"How awful," she said. "He must be terrified. I'll do what I can to help. See you soon."

Ty said goodbye and was about half a mile from Little Falls when he heard the familiar exhaust note of Thurston's truck.

Thurston was very agitated. "Ty, I saw the most amazing thing this evening. You're not going to believe it. I don't even believe it myself. I'm almost worried that if I tell you this you're going to think I need to see a shrink."

Ty told Thurston not to worry and listened with rapt attention as Thurston related Jasper's capture as seen from inside the house.

When Thurston finished, the two sat in silence for a moment. Ty took a deep breath. "What do you think should be done with this guy, Jasper, who was captured?"

"He should be freed, whatever it takes. The poor guy is terrified. I don't know who or what he is but he should be let go. If there are more of these gnome things living around us they may have some mischief in them but they obviously aren't trying to hurt anybody. They shouldn't be put in some kind of freak show."

"I agree," Ty said as they approached the bottom of his road. Did Big Mike give any more details about how he wants to run this carnival show tomorrow?"

"All I know is that he plans to call more TV stations and newspapers, telling them we have a gnome to show at Roscoe's Campground up the mountain off the road to Paw Paw. He wants to charge $5 a person for people to see Jasper one at a time in a walk-through tent. Roscoe will have his camp store open to sell snacks, soda, and barbecue."

"Thanks," Ty said, as Thurston slowed to turn up to Ty's cabin. "I can hop out here and walk up." At this cue, the gnomes quietly crawled out from under the tarp and scrambled down over the side, off into the shadows.

Thurston stopped the truck and took a deep breath. "That little Jasper fellow helped me out. I'm worried for him. You can't just kidnap someone and exploit him. Good grief."

"I'm sure it will all work out," Ty said, climbing out of the truck. "Are you going to go out to Roscoe's yourself to see how it all unfolds?"

"Yeah, I'll be out there at 10 a.m."

Ty waved goodbye and started walking up to his cabin. When he was halfway up, he heard the unmistakable low rumble and gear changes of a tractor trailer scaling a steep grade. Ty grinned and started jogging down to the river. A few minutes later he saw a truck rounding a bend, headlights sweeping the tall oaks lining the road.

A head popped out on the passenger's side. "Ty, it's me Marvin, all the way from Wyoming – me, Anna my beautiful cowgirl, and Midnight. I should not be shouting but I'm so excited."

Midnight barked and whined, then scrambled over Marvin's lap and out onto the dirt road. Ty leaned down to greet him, just as Midnight launched himself, hitting Ty full in the chest.

The Indian driver, Ben, climbed down from the cab and introduced himself, as did Anna, the last to exit the truck. Ty shook hands with them and marveled at the unusual group. "It's wonderful to see you all. I'm so happy everything worked out so well. Would you like to come up to the cabin to have something to eat?"

Ben thanked Ty for the offer but said he needed to drive on to Roanoke before he got too tired.

"But we'll stop in and visit a spell with you, you old galoot," Marvin told Ty.

Ty smiled at Ben. "Have you been teaching Marvin how to talk cowboy?"

"Well, he sure talks the talk. But you know, he actually is a pretty quick learner. He can track a bit.

He can even rope a cow if it's not moving."

Ben said goodbye and backed up Ty's dirt road, making a three-point turn to head back out the river road.

Moments later, Ty's heart leapt at seeing Casey's Subaru crest the hill and pull over to let Ben pass. Casey parked at the bottom of the hill and jogged over to the others, where Marvin introduced Anna to Casey.

Casey said hello and forced a smile. But her look was stricken. "Have you heard the news on the radio? The announcers on a Frederick station are having a field day, laughing it up about how some local good ole boy has caught a gnome. Come listen."

The four reached Casey's car just in time to hear the latest report.

"Folks, we've got a reporter on the scene in the town of Little Falls, West Virginia. Go ahead, Frank, tell us what's going on there."

"Well Joe, this is unreal. There are four TV trucks along the road, many radio and print reporters here, plus a growing crowd of onlookers from miles away. And this is all in hope of seeing a gnome. As we reported earlier, photo experts have studied the photo taken by the Warm Springs reporter. They say there's no sign the photo has been manipulated."

"The photo aside, do all these people really think gnomes are real, for goodness sakes?"

The reporter said most people suspected the gnome sighting was a hoax but others swore there had been sightings for years of odd little figures in the local mountains. Meanwhile, the police had cordoned off the house with yellow tape and been arguing with the homeowner, known as "Big Mike."

"The cops want to go into the house, concerned it's a hostage situation. But Big Mike is refusing to let them in. He's coming out of the house again to talk. Let's see if we can catch the audio."

Big Mike stepped onto the front porch, raising a hand to shield his eyes from the bright TV lights. "The cops don't have a warrant but they want me to let them into my house to make sure there's no hostage. But they're also telling me they think I'm crazy for believing in gnomes. Well if there are no gnomes, then I've got no hostage and they should all just leave me alone."

Many onlookers and several of the police officers chuckled at this.

"If you all want to see who or what I've got to show you, come on up to Roscoe's Campground out the Paw Paw road starting at 10 a.m. tomorrow. You can see for yourselves, $5 for adults, $2 for kids. You might as well all go on home now. I'm going to bed. There won't be anything to see unless you come out to Roscoe's tomorrow."

Big Mike walked into his house and closed the door.

The TV crews started packing up their equipment and driving away. The last TV reporter on hand turned to his cameraman. "Well, folks, I think that's it for the evening. Tune in tomorrow when we'll be broadcasting live from Roscoe's. Whether it's a gnome or a huge hoax, it's a big story either way."

Ty groaned. "It's Jasper, that's been caught, I'm afraid. Gnome One has called an emergency meeting up at the cavern."

Ty said he'd been just about to break the bad news when Casey pulled up. "Marvin and Anna, I'm sorry this has spoiled your homecoming."

Anna shook her head. "Not to worry, rescuing Jasper is what's most important right now."

The four of them plus Midnight walked up the hill in silence, still stunned at the night's turn of events. They stopped at Ty's cabin to leave some luggage, so they could make better time climbing to the cavern to join the meeting.

The hike was made easier by the moon, bright enough to see by even under tree cover. As they approached the cavern, Ty stopped. "I don't know the way from here. We wore hoods from here on."

Marvin stepped to the front. "No time for hoods. I dub you official friends of the gnomes. There's supposed to be a ceremony to go along with it and a bunch of signatures. We can do all that later. For now it means full speed ahead."

Within a few minutes, they walked into the cavern and initially escaped notice because of the mayhem within. The little gnomies were running amok. Throngs of them, not more than knee high on a biggie, were chasing around the cavern with fierce expressions and executing swift leg kicks and karate chops in the air.

"Who are we going to get?" one yelled.

"Big Mike!" came the thunderous reply.

A moment later, a buzz started with much excited elbowing and pointing by gnomes of all sizes. The new arrivals had been spotted. New cries went up.

Gnome Mountain

"It's prince Ty and princess Casey!"

"The biggie royal couple have returned!"

Ty and Casey waved, embarrassed by the deafening welcome. Ty stepped aside and pointed to Marvin and Anna. "Here are the real guests of honor, back from the wilds of Wyoming, cowgirl Anna and cowboy Marvin."

At this, more rounds of applause broke out and many little gnomies started dancing and hopping, spinning pretend lassos overhead and giving each other horseback rides. Meanwhile, an exasperated Gnome One raised his hand.

"Silence," he pleaded. Reluctantly, the crowd quieted, turning to Gnome One.

"I, too, am delighted at the return of Anna, Marvin, Casey, and Ty. They deserve the fine welcome and we'll have other festivities in their honor, I promise you. But now we must grapple with this great challenge, the rescue of poor gnome Jasper, is locked in a fortified house and homemade cell in Little Falls. Unless we can rescue him, he will be put on public display and our quiet, peaceful life will be ruined forever."

Gnome One called on the audience to focus and bring forth their best ideas for a rescue. "We'll break into groups of ten. Each group will select a leader and he or she will write up a rescue plan with the help of the group. In half an hour, each group will present its plan and the senior council will decide which one to use. Please organize and get started."

Amazingly, the rowdy bunch started working as instructed. Gnome One looked on approvingly, then

163

turned to Casey and Ty. "We'll sort this out. You go back to your cabins and get some rest. We'll meet you at the bottom of your road at 7 a.m. I expect we'll have roles for you. Are you willing to take part? We won't ask you to do anything that breaks biggie laws."

Casey and Ty looked at each other and nodded. Ty then turned back to Gnome One. "Sure," he said.

Minutes later, the two of them were headed down the mountain. Ty walked Casey to her cabin, gave her a quick hug, then turned to walk home.

Casey sighed. "I'm worried about tomorrow."

Ty stopped and looked back. "Me, too, but I've learned not to underestimate the gnomies. Imagine unleashing just the little ones. They'd chase Big Mike into next week."

Casey laughed. "Well it'll be a show tomorrow of some kind, that's for sure. I'll meet you at the bottom of your road at 7 a.m."

Ty nodded. "Okay, see you then."

CHAPTER 10

The gnomes worked efficiently overnight. At Gnome One's instruction, the little gnomies had retrieved cardboard and twine from the workshop's shipping area and fashioned masks. Each youngster had been instructed to draw a face resembling his or her own.

The process went surprisingly well, without a single fight. True, there were some taunts, mostly one gnomie looking at another's drawing and saying something like, "Please, that makes you look handsome. Make it realistic."

Gnome One and several others walked their bikes down the mountain, roused Ty, fetched him his bike from the shed, and rode out the river road to visit Daryl at Jimmy's Garage.

The gnomes had detailed their plan to Ty and promised he'd be back home within an hour. Ty and the others found Daryl asleep behind the wheel of his truck. His soft snoring was the only sound on the garage lot, aside from the buzzing of insects under the streetlight.

The gnomes caught a break. Normally, Daryl's parents would have come to fetch him but they had left town for the weekend while Daryl stayed behind to work at the garage. This made it easy to enlist Daryl's help.

When the group of cycling gnomes arrived, they listened in from the shadows beside the cinderblock garage.

Ty walked up to Daryl's truck and nudged Daryl awake through the driver's side window. "Hi Daryl, my name is Ty. You know about this guy Big Mike who's supposed to be showing off a gnome out at Roscoe's tomorrow?"

Daryl yawned and nodded. "Sure you couldn't miss all the lights, police, and activity last night. Really put us on the map."

"Well, I've got a bunch of kids from a camp up on the mountain who are desperate to see this gnome, but we have no way to transport them. I hear you own that old school bus out back. Is it running?"

"Yeah, I've got a guy up at Capon Bridge who wants to run canoe shuttles with it. I've got it running fine, just need to paint green over the school bus yellow."

"Great. How'd you like to make two hundred dollars, driving my campers to and from this gnome show at Roscoe's tomorrow?"

Daryl brightened. "I could do that, sure."

"I'll have my kids ready and down at the second low-water bridge by seven thirty. You drive us out to Roscoe's and back and you'll have money in your pocket and still get back to your garage before opening time."

Daryl stuck out his hand. "It's a deal."

As they shook hands, Daryl added, "Don't worry about me not waking up on time. As much as I fall asleep during the day and evening, I'm up and out of bed early in the morning. No worries there."

Daryl started his truck and drove off in one direction, while Ty and the gnomes saddled up and rode off in the other.

Gnome One rode level with Ty and patted him on the back. "Well done, Ty. You'll be back in bed shortly and all we need is for you and Casey to herd the kids on and off the bus. Can you get her to join you by the bridge at seven thirty?"

Ty nodded. "Of course, she and I are eager to help any way we can."

Casey stopped by Ty's cabin in the morning. He poured her a cup of coffee and told her about the arrangements he'd made with Daryl for driving the bus. "I'm afraid that's all I know about their plans."

At seven thirty they were down on the river road and looked in awe at the ranks of gnomes striding solemnly downhill. Leading the group were Gnome One and the other elders, followed by the little gnomies and their parents. All wore traditional gnome outfits of pointy red caps, green tunics, and brown pants. The youngsters carried the masks they'd made the night before.

Gnome One pulled Casey and Ty aside and whispered instructions to them earnestly. Both nodded when he was finished. "You can count on us Gnome One," Ty said. And as Gnome One walked away, Ty and Casey chuckled and looked at each other wide eyed.

Soon the two biggies and gnomes heard the rumble of a school bus. The parents and elders hugged the little ones, then quickly melted into the woods.

The gnomies donned their masks and chatted excitedly amongst themselves. Such was their excitement at doing what biggie kids do five days a week – board and ride a yellow school bus.

Daryl brought the bus to a halt and stared in disbelief at the array of gnomes.

"Swing out the stop sign," one yelled. "We need to be safe."

Daryl complied and the gnomies cheered.

Casey stood by the open door. "Alright, children, use your walking feet and keep your hands to yourselves when you sit down."

Ty smiled. She's got a teacher's knack with kids, he thought. And she'll need it with this bunch.

After everyone was seated, Daryl shut the doors, turned the bus around and headed back toward town. Daryl glanced in the rear view mirror, then turned to Ty. "The kids all look a little sinister with those masks."

Ty patted Daryl on the shoulder. "Oh not at all. They're just huge gnome fans. This happens to be gnome week at camp, so the kids are really excited."

"Gnome week? Man I'd hardly ever thought of gnomes and now in just two days we've had a gnome supposedly caught by Big Mike right here in Little Falls. Plus, suddenly you've got all these kids crazy about gnomes."

Casey turned to the gnomes and noticed they'd started getting antsy. "Let's sing some of our camp songs."

The gnomes started happily belting out perennial camp favorites like *Oh Susannah, Camptown Racetrack*, and *My Darling Clementine*. Between the songs and corny jokes, the drive went quickly and they soon climbed a steep grade on a rutted dirt road and passed through the gate of Roscoe's Campground.

The hilltop campground featured a panoramic view of the opposite ridge, home to gnome cavern. By bus on the serpentine road, the trip had taken thirty minutes. The trip took just five minutes as a bird flies, the bird in this case being Talon, friend to gnomes and lover of deer jerky.

Talon settled high in a lone pine towering above the campground. A bath house and camp store stood to the side edged with woods. Opposite, tent sites overlooked the river canyon.

Beside the campground road stood a large, covered shelter with twelve picnic tables and a stone fireplace. In the very center, long panels of overlapping camo cloth hung from the roof's timbers, creating what looked like a huge hunting blind.

Attached to the cloth, facing the road was a large hand-lettered sign saying "Line Up Here To View The Gnome."

Three cars were parked on the road, level with the stage. The bus parked and Ty could see Roscoe and Big Mike chatting and looking up at the sound of the buses' motor.

Roscoe pointed and grinned. "We're not even

supposed to open for another two hours and already we've got a whole busload of young customers. This looks very promising."

Big Mike approached the bus and peered at the faces inside. "Look at them. They're all in full gnome costume, same as our friend Jasper. Who knew there were so many gnome lovers?"

Daryl opened the door and Casey stepped out, motioning to the kids to follow her. "Go run around in the woods to play for a bit but don't wander off. I'll see if these nice men will let you see the gnome early. So stay within earshot."

"Also, keep your masks on so the gnome will see how you've honored him by dressing like gnomes today," Ty added.

As the kids scampered off into the woods, a state trooper pulled up in his cruiser and gaped at the disappearing horde of kids. He climbed out of his vehicle and turned to Ty. "Wow, those kids are going all out for this gnome thing, huh?"

"They sure are, sir." Ty added innocently, "Are you expecting trouble here today officer?"

"Nah, dispatch just asked me to come out and keep an eye on things. What with all the TV trucks and publicity from last night, I'm sure it'll be busy here, that's all. We'll likely need to do some crowd control and pull in more officers, maybe put up some barricades. These local boys don't have any idea what they've started."

"I'd imagine not." Ty glanced downhill and was surprised to see Lisa arriving in her old truck. Sighting over her shoulder, he noticed a slight movement beneath the tarp in the back of her truck.

Ty jogged over to Lisa and gestured toward the figures in the truck bed. "Lisa, how did you get roped into this?"

"No thanks to you," she said. "Here are these delightful men living just up the mountain from me and you've kept them a secret?"

"Well, I think they like to reveal themselves to us biggies if and when they choose."

"Apparently, last around midnight they decided would be a good time to make my acquaintance. I'd never woken up before to the rapping of little gnome knuckles on my bedroom window. They explained they were friends of yours and that they knew about my acting classes from seeing us heading off to the Art Haus together. They said they needed me to impersonate someone to foil a kidnapping."

A rustling sound came from the back and Gnome One poked his head out. "Ty, trust us," he hissed. "We've got this all figured out. Just let the plan unfold. We'll tell you all the details later."

"Okay, good luck, everyone," he said, stepping away from the truck and watching Lisa walk up to the state trooper.

"Hello officer," she said. "Do you know where I could find Big Mike and Roscoe?"

"They must be in that tent in the picnic shelter."

Lisa nodded and walked to the tent, parted two panels of cloth and slipped inside. In front of her was Jasper, sitting cross legged and dejected. He was locked in a portable kennel box, the walls made of stout chromed wire. Next to Jasper were Big Mike and

Roscoe, happily debating how much money they might make that day. Both men looked up, eyes wide at Lisa's good looks.

"Gentlemen, my name is Cindy Jones, I'm a paralegal for Lawn Ornament Enterprises. We have a contract with Jasper Jones here to do appearances at trade shows where we demonstrate our lawn figures and other decorations. Mr. Jones was the winner of our nationwide 'Most Gnome Like' competition. He does look very convincing, wouldn't you agree?"

Big Mike nodded. "Without a doubt."

"Well, I assume you have an appearance contract with him for this event of yours?"

Big Mike looked at the ground. "Of course."

"Then you know, Jasper can only appear in the open, looking his happy, gnome-like self, not like some miserable caged beast?"

Roscoe and Big Mike exchanged a worried glance.

Lisa leveled her eyes on Jasper next. "Jasper, you showed poor judgment to agree to this sad spectacle. But we can compromise here. Is everyone okay with Jasper appearing outside the tent under the picnic shelter with nobody other than visitors within six feet?"

Roscoe and Big Mike looked at each, nodded, then turned back to Lisa. "Yes, that would be fine."

Jasper nodded, too. "Trust me I was very much against the tent and cage idea myself. It's most demeaning. I'm glad you've straightened this out."

The new ground rules in place, Big Mike released Jasper from his cage and the group emerged from the blind to stand on the slab floor of the picnic shelter, which overlooked a field and the river valley beyond.

Casey had been watching the blind closely. Once Jasper was in view, she quickly called the gnomies, asking them to form a single-file line. Commotion ensued as the gnomies came streaming out of the woods and milled about, before lining themselves up as requested.

With this diversion, Gnome One slithered on his belly toward the back of Lisa's pickup. Still under the tarp, he reached his hand out, released the tailgate, and dropped silently to the ground. Nate and Marvin followed quickly.

Keeping their heads down, they fished some long, narrow tote bags out of the back and disappeared into the cover of the dense woods. From there, they worked their way fifty yards to the last of the trees, level with the edge of the rock outcropping jutting out over the valley.

They hurriedly assembled their supplies and looked back toward the picnic shelter. To their relief, everyone else in the campground stood staring intently at Jasper. Adding to the distraction, the gnomies cheered wildly to see Jasper safe and sound.

Casey gave a quick look at Jasper. "On the count of three, let's all shout a good 'Hip, Hip, Hooray' for Jasper, okay?"

The gnomies all nodded and yelled eagerly. Then on the last yell of "Hooray," the gnomies erupted. They pounced on Big Mike and Roscoe, knocking and holding them down. In that instant, Jasper bolted for the cliff while Gnome One, Ty, and Nate seized the wood and nylon contraption they'd assembled, and set it jutting out over the cliff's edge.

Alas, Big Mike and Roscoe had freed themselves from the gnomies and were closing in on Jasper, who'd abandoned his all-out sprint for an apparent limp. But that wasn't it. He was fishing for something in his pants pocket. Just as his pursuers closed within a few feet, Jasper produced his leather pouch, and darted off in a fresh burst of speed.

At the cliff's edge, Gnome One was briefly triumphant. In record time, they'd fitted together one of Granddad Travis' hang gliders, ready for Jasper's flight to safety. But Big Mike and Roscoe were fast on Jasper's heels, sure to capture him before he could don his harness, grab the control bar, and fly free.

But Jasper had one last card to play. He threw his right arm skyward, sending a fistful of deer jerky high in the air. Talon, his head already turned sideways in anticipation, came plummeting out of his tree, razor sharp talons extended below him. Terrified, Big Mike and Roscoe dove to the ground, covering their heads with their arms. Jasper stopped, turned back, and dropped one more piece of deer jerky on each man's back.

"Be gentle now," Jasper admonished Talon.

The hawk obliged, hopping onto Big Mike's back and lifting the piece of jerky to his mouth. Big Mike squirmed then yelped as the majestic bird applied gentle pressure with his feet. Learning from this example, Roscoe lay completely still, quivering. He had no interest in experiencing the pain that caused a tough man like Big Mike to whimper in agony.

His pursuers detained, Jasper jogged to the rim,

donned his harness and helmet, and grabbed the control bar. He ran the few steps out and over the cliff's edge and soon banked into wide spiraling turns.

Shortly afterward, Ty was joined by Big Mike and Roscoe to watch Jasper's descent, the two men having jumped to their feet once Talon flew back to his perch with the last of his deer jerky.

"Oh my, that is awesome," Big Mike said in wonder, his fury subsiding. "But where the heck is that little guy going to land? There ain't nothing but steep woods and trees down there and he can't be making those big sweeping turns where the valley's no wider than the river."

Roscoe nodded, still catching his breath. "And he's all rigged into that glider thing. He lands in the water and the weight will push him under. Man, I'm feeling bad we put the poor little guy in this danger."

Roscoe turned to Ty. "We just wanted to make a few bucks out here, not get somebody killed. Good grief."

Big Mike nodded. "Yeah, I kinda liked the guy. He was a handful alright, and he cost me some money. I just wanted to make my money back and then some. We were gonna let him go. He knew that."

Lisa had quietly come up beside the others and stood watching, too. "Good grief, you see what he's going to try to do, don't you?"

"What?" the others said in unison.

"He's going to try to land on the low-water bridge! And that's single lane, maybe eight feet across."

Big Mike grinned. "Ten bucks says he makes it. That guy's got spirit. I'll tell you that."

Ty shook his head. "Who's gonna take that bet? You

think anybody wants to root for him drowning in the river? But I'm glad you're pulling for him."

Lisa squinted. "Rats, we're losing him in the fog rising off the river. The wind's shifting and you can't even see the bridge now. And he must be making his final turn, he's so low over the water."

Meanwhile Casey, the little gnomies still in their masks, and everyone else at the campground had come crowding along the cliff's edge to watch.

Suddenly a huge roar went up. Jasper had come into view, his hang glider headed dead center over the single-lane bridge.

For Jasper, the landing was hardly as promising as it looked from above. A blustery wind over the river buffeted him off course. He'd never make the bridge now.

Jasper momentarily let go of the control bar and released the buckle holding the harness to his chest. The hang glider lurched partly free, banked sharply, caught a wing in the water and flipped.

The crowd on the cliff sounded a collective gasp, unable to tell whether Jasper had been thrown free or pinned underwater. At that distance it was impossible to tell a swimmer's head from the rocks that dotted the river.

It would take a biggie at least a minute to swim to the bank from the middle of the river. But who knew whether gnomes swim well or swim at all? The waiting was miserable. At least two minutes went by.

Then among the onlookers, a murmur went up. Could that be a figure emerging from the water? A few moments later, there against the light planks of the bridge's decking was a figure running back and forth on the bridge, waving his arms in the air. A huge cheer went up from the cliff. Jasper had made it to safety.

Having witnessed the safe landing, the crowd slowly dispersed, filing off to their vehicles. The little gnomies were a challenge, however. Overcome with excitement at Jasper's daring escape, they'd stuck their arms out like little pilots themselves. They ran, rocked their arms up and down, and did forward and back flips.

Most distressing to Ty and Casey was the prospect of the gnomies' masks falling off and the kids being discovered for the real gnomes they were. When a stray mask did fall loose, Casey would quickly scoop up the barefaced youngster and carry him or her aboard the bus.

Daryl sat in the driver's seat, his mouth agape. "I'm not even going to ask," he muttered.

Ty called out to Big Mike and Roscoe. "Guys, Jasper's people want everyone to forgive and forget. They're going to make up for your poker losses and some of the money you missed out on today."

Ty shook hands with both men, then turned back to the idling bus.

"Hey Ty," Big Mike called out. "You see that Jasper fellow before we do, please tell him we've got no hard feelings, at least we won't once he's paid us back."

"Will do."

Ty boarded the bus and Daryl drove out through the campground gate just as three TV trucks came up the mountain. The driver of the first truck motioned to the bus to stop and rolled down his window. "What's with that load of kids you've got dressed up like gnomes? Why are they headed away? Did the show start early?"

Ty nodded. "Yeah, I'm afraid you missed it. There was a guy there who looked a whole lot like a gnome. He said his name was Jasper. You can ask people up there that are getting ready to leave. They'll tell you they saw him, too. He escaped, though, I'm afraid. It's all over."

"You're pulling my leg buddy, no need to be a wise guy."

Ty shook his head. "Nope, that's really what happened. I do feel bad for you guys, though. I can imagine you go on the air with that story and people will think you've either fallen for a hoax or are in on it, too."

The driver and the reporter next to him shook their heads in disgust. "These crazy country fellas up here," said the reporter. "They've got too much time on their hands, pulling crazy stunts like this. Why can't it be simple like the state fair, where you know the county's biggest pumpkin or fattest hog is sure going to be there when you roll up?"

"Better luck next time," Ty said, as Daryl resumed the drive.

Meanwhile, Lisa, Gnome One, and Jasper had already reached Little Falls. She pulled her truck up behind Big Mike's house, reached under the tarp and produced the wooden J2, Jasper's look alike. She hung an envelope around its neck and left it on Big Mike's back steps, where he'd see it walking in from his driveway.

"There's his money," Gnome One said, nodding.

A few miles on, Daryl downshifted to slow the bus as it descended to the low-water bridge.

"Please stop and let Casey and me out here," Ty said. "I'll jog over in a minute and meet you at the other side. I see something I need to do."

Ty ran down the steps and out the door. Casey following, he rock hopped through a pool in the river to a brush-covered island in the middle of the river. There he saw a cloth-covered corner of Jasper's hang glider, just barely visible behind a thicket of sycamore saplings.

With Casey's help, they quickly disassembled the small craft and carried the canopy and frame pieces back to the bus, where they deposited it in the aisle, to the cheers of the little ones.

Daryl drove the bus back to the bottom of Ty's road, dropped off the gnomies and their "camp counselors," and turned the bus around.

Ty reached up to Daryl's window holding a white envelope in his arm. "Here's the two hundred bucks we agreed on. Thanks so much, Daryl."

Daryl chuckled. "I'll take the money like we agreed. But you know, I would have done that run for free just for the experience. I'm still not quite sure I believe all that I saw today but it sure was something."

"I hear you. I'm still reeling from it myself," Ty said, patting the fender of the bus as Daryl pulled away.

Once the bus was out of sight, the gnome parents came out from their hiding places to fetch and hug their kids. Just a few moments later, one of the gnomies yelled, having spotted a soggy Jasper walking toward them through the woods. Accompanying him were Gnome One and Nate, who'd waited for him further north on the path, near Lisa's.

The biggies and gnomies all raced through the trees to hug him and clap Jasper and the others on the back. "I heard your bus," Jasper said. "I figured though that I'd stay off the road on the way back from the bridge. I've had enough excitement for one day and didn't want to be seen by anyone else."

The gnomes said their goodbyes and started back into the woods, heading up to the cavern. Gnome One turned back and yelled, "Remember, we meet at sundown for the party at the ridge."

"We'll be there," Ty shouted. He turned to Casey. "Want to come up for a sandwich?"

"Sure."

Ty put his arm around Casey's shoulder. "Is this okay?"

She turned and smiled. "Yeah, it's fine," she said, putting an arm around his waist. Back at the cabin they ate lunch, both yawning as they talked.

Ty took a deep breath. "I'm beat after all that tension and excitement. How about you?"

"I was thinking exactly the same thing. A nap's indicated, I'd say."

Ty took off his shoes and sat on the bed. "Want to join me? I'll be a perfect gentleman, honest."

Casey hesitated. "Alright. But you have to keep your word. My parents have made clear that if I'm not on my best behavior they won't ever let me come out here on my own again."

"Don't worry. That's the last thing I want, to have

them mad at me or for me not to be able to see you."

Casey took off her shoes, lay down next to Ty and they slept for an hour. Afterward, Casey went back to her cabin, changed into a swimsuit and t-shirt and met Ty and Midnight at the river. They'd been there just a few minutes when they saw Lisa pull up and carry a tube down to the river to join them.

The three of them lazed happily in the warm river for much of the afternoon, chatting and recalling the details of the day's adventures. Midnight enjoyed himself, too, fetching sticks and snapping at minnows in the water.

A family with two children was sitting on a sandbar in the shallows beside the canoe launch. The parents hailed Ty and Casey on one of their many circuits walking upriver on the road and floating back down.

"Did you hear to the radio this morning?" the dad called out.

"No, why?" Ty replied.

"There was some crazy story about a guy in a gnome outfit hang gliding down from the ridge across the river. Some people even swore the guy didn't just look like a gnome. They said he was a *real* gnome."

Ty laughed and turned to the kids, who looked to be about eight and ten. "That would be really cool, wouldn't it guys, to see a gnome?" The kids nodded eagerly, eyes wide.

Ty turned back to the dad. "I'm sorry I missed hearing about it on the radio. I'll tune in when I get back to the cabin. Thanks for the tip."

Casey and Ty walked in silence until they were out of earshot. Casey then leaned over, "You danced your way out of that one pretty nicely."

"Well it's true. I didn't hear a thing on the radio."

After swimming, the three friends went back to their cabins, showered, and met up again at dusk to hike up to the gnomes' party. Ty looked at the others as they started up the dirt road. "This ought to be an evening to remember."

They bypassed the turn to the gnome cavern and continued straight up to top of the ridge, stopping now and then to admire the sun bathing them and the surrounding woods in vivid orange light. Lisa turned to face downhill. "It's so beautiful up here."

Ty nodded. "Any time I head uphill for a walk around sunset, I can't help myself. I always hike farther than I'd planned. Did either of you bring flashlights or headlamps? I've got extras in here," he said, pointing to his daypack.

It was getting dark as they reached the top of the ridge but they found the gnomes easily, by walking toward the blue-gray plume of wood smoke gently curling up through the trees. The adults and little gnomies already cooking sausages over the fire.

Gnome One, Marvin, Jasper, Nate, and all the other gnomes they knew were there, plus plenty more. "Come have some bratwurst we get fresh from Wisconsin," said Gnome One.

Ty stared. "From Wisconsin? How on earth do you pull that off?"

"We sell mail order. We buy mail order. Most food we buy boxed, if we can't grow it ourselves. Fresh meat we buy packed in dry ice. We get it home the usual way, jumping pickups of people we know. We've got some fresh potato salad and canned sauerkraut, too. You know we gnomes originally come from Germany, right?"

Ty hesitated. "I knew the first books about gnomes were written in Germany. No offense, but I thought they were myths, up there with Siegfried killing the dragon at the Drachenfels, that sort of thing."

Gnome One sighed. "Ah, it's criminal that such basic history isn't known by the kids of today. Thank goodness we have our own schools to teach what's really important. Anyway, tuck in while the food's hot. It's time to celebrate!"

Pandemonium broke loose, as it always does at gnome parties. Little gnomies did skits. Some jumped recklessly over the fire. Some leapt from one tree to another and many, still in awe of the day's hang gliding, were buzzing around, flapping their arms, and making whooshing sounds.

Just as the antics were winding down, the gnome elders dug away at the fire pit and retrieved a vast Dutch oven of simmering peach cobbler. This led to many gnomies devouring the searing hot dessert, then running around frantically, huffing and puffing to cool their scorched mouths.

Gnome One called for everyone's attention. "Let's hear some stories from those with adventures to tell. Marvin please go first."

Marvin rose to his feet, bowed, and extended his hand to Anna to stand alongside him, this small act of chivalry drawing loud applause.

Marvin raised an arm to call for silence. "Well, my gnomies, you know I have been fretting, pondering, plotting, and teeth gnashing since my beloved Anna forsook me for cowgirling out west. I believe you all know how she saved my life as a young boy."

"Yes, yes," cried an old crone. "We've heard that story ever since you were a little pup with just one snaggle tooth. Tell us only the new stuff."

Marvin's eyes narrowed in annoyance. "Okay, so my dear biggie friend Ty chauffeured me in the fantastic Chevelle convertible clear out to Wyoming. We learned about great horse leaps, about President Lincoln, about wonderful ice creams, about Lewis and Clark, about cowboying, tracking, and camping."

"I asked many things of the Internet and it answered me very well. So when Ty left to take the Chevelle to the owner, Midnight and I went a sniffin' and a prowlin' and lookin' high and lookin' low for Anna. I called to her. I made signs. I tried many things, but I found no Anna."

"Then one time at night, I made a big search with Midnight using his sniffer and we came to a huge rock formation making a big spooky shadow and with bushes all around in the dead of night. We could smell smoke and hear a fire cracking and popping. I saw the horses tied up and they were little Shetland ponies. That meant it had to be little gnome cow punchers!"

"I was so excited I forgot about hiding and ran out from behind my bush yelling like a crazy gnome, 'Anna, Anna, it's me, your gnomie Marvin from West Virginia.'" But my yelling scared them and they were frightened, too. Anna threw her lasso and roped me like a runaway calf. Now I was scared, too. Just to be safe I yelled, "I am not a calf. Don't catch me and brand my hind parts. I was not very brave."

Marvin then related how he had courted Anna, singing cowboy songs he'd learned from the Internet and saying nice sweet things in her ear. So after a while she had said she'd come back home, riding in the truck of a friend, an American Indian.

Marvin smiled at Anna. "So it was all very happy and Anna is wonderful."

The gnomes cheered at the tale's conclusion and begged for more.

Gnome One called on Ty. "You go next, tell us your story."

Ty rose to his feet and hesitated, not knowing how to begin.

"Tell us about you and princess Casey," one little girl yelled.

"Well, I'm afraid Casey is not really my princess."

The little girl leapt to her feet and balled up her tiny fist. "You have a different princess?"

"No, no! Casey is the one I'd most like to have as my princess in the whole wide world. But she is not my princess yet."

"What have you done to try to make her your princess?"

Ty sighed. "Little girl you have a lot of questions. Okay, we have great talks, we go swimming and canoeing together, and we hiked the Abandoned Turnpike together."

"Boring," shouted the girl.

Ty noticed Casey's face. She was laughing hysterically. Ty grimaced and looked back at the girl. "Well little girl, what should I do?"

"Kiss her, you idiot!"

Ty grinned. "Casey, could you come join me for a moment?"

Casey paused for a moment, leapt to her feet, ran over to Ty, threw her arms around his neck, and kissed him hard on the lips.

"Now that's more like it," shouted the little girl, as the crowd erupted in cheers.

Finally, the party wound down at about 9 p.m. and everyone started for home.

Casey, Lisa, and Ty walked down the road together, still able to see by the moonlight through the clearing over the road.

Ty stopped. "You know I need to make a call while we still have a cell signal."

"So do I," said Casey.

"Me, too," said Lisa.

Ty checked his phone and found he had several missed calls from his dad. He immediately dialed home and learned his dad had found a buyer for the bar and would clear enough money to buy a house in a better part of town. More good news, an old friend of his dad's was opening an upscale restaurant and wanted to hire Ty's dad as the manager.

Ty shared the good news with Casey and Lisa and asked the girls what news they had.

Casey laughed. "My dad wanted to know about the great gnome prank. He said the TV and radio stations back home had a field day with it, said the locals must have really played a great prank."

"How about you, Lisa, any news on your end?"

Lisa hesitated. "I'm a bit embarrassed to admit this,

but I finally broke down and returned a call to Vincent."

"Vincent?" Ty and Casey said, amazed.

"Yeah, he told me he realized what a jerk he'd been and asked whether he could take me out to dinner, have me tell him exactly all the issues he's got, and say what he should do about them."

Lisa said she'd told him that if this was a ruse, it would get him nowhere. She said she knew bad acting better than anyone. But Vincent had promised he was sincere and just really wanted to learn how to behave.

Ty grimaced. "Please tell me you're not going to reform him so he can steal Casey back, I mean not that she's mine exactly, of course."

Lisa laughed. "Not to worry, Ty. He knows he's lost Casey and, frankly, he says he's now in love with me and if I can't love him back at least I can teach him how to treat the next girl. You know I like drama. So, that's why I agreed to dinner with him."

"Wow," Ty said and looked at Casey, who was shaking her head. "There's nothing but surprises these days."

Casey and Ty walked Lisa to her cabin, then continued on to Casey's.

Ty and Casey stood on the front porch enjoying the quiet of the night and watching a mass of fireflies flickering over a grassy stretch of riverbank.

Ty turned to her. "I think I'm going to have to insist on a hug and a kiss. Otherwise, I don't think I can face that bossy little girl again."

Casey laughed and put her arms around his neck. "I don't dare disappoint that girl either. And, seriously, I thank you for being patient with me."

"Of course. I couldn't be any happier."

"Me, too," Casey said.

Casey agreed to pick Ty up at 8 a.m. to drive back to Baltimore. "Sure, I know how eager you are to celebrate your dad's good news."

CHAPTER 11

Casey rolled up in the Subaru on time to find Ty and Midnight playing a game of fetch in the driveway, Ty's duffel bag packed and sitting on the porch.

Ty and Midnight quickly climbed in and they were soon passing through Warm Springs and driving to Hancock.

Ty peered down at the railroad tracks. "It's hard to believe a certain gnome was lying flat on his back atop an open coal car on his way to peek in your window." They both laughed at the image.

"You know that's one more good reason to stick together," Ty said. "Otherwise, who could we talk to about the cavern, the crazy gnomes, and their carrying on? Nobody would believe us."

Casey shot Ty a sly look. "Oh, I don't know, I could see Big Mike and me sitting in rocking chairs on his porch talking about deer jerky and hang gliders. There'd be quite a bit to say."

Ty huffed. "I'm going to insist on something right now. If you dump me for another guy, you've got to promise me that it's not Big Mike. That I couldn't take, though he's not so bad after all."

Casey nodded. "And I can't see throwing you over for a gnome. I have to admit, those gnomes can be a bit trying, if they're messing with you. Never mind that they're like that with each other, too. They're probably bitter that they don't have magic or super powers to work with. They're more like Batman than Superman. They're earthbound, blue collar."

"Exactly, they're like Larry the Cable Guy or Jeff Foxworthy, just smaller."

In Hagerstown, they stopped for gas and Ty took the opportunity to call Thurston and ask for a couple days off. He explained he needed to help his dad for a few days.

Thurston had no objection. "I don't have any jobs stacked up at the moment. I can just knock 'em out one at a time and then pick up the pace when you get back. Say hi to your dad for me."

An hour later, Casey pulled the car up in front of the Chesapeake Tavern.

Ty climbed out of the car and walked up to the tavern door, Casey at his side. They walked in to find Walt reading the newspaper and drinking coffee.

Walt spotted them first, leapt to his feet, and rushed over to throw an arm around both Ty and Casey. "I'm so glad to see you."

Casey stayed to chat for few minutes, then rose to leave. "Call me later, Ty, okay?"

Ty nodded, "Definitely. Let me come get my stuff

and poor Midnight. We left him in the car."

Ty called Casey later that evening. "Casey," he blurted out, "what are you doing tomorrow morning?"

"Nothing, why?

"Do you want to come house hunting with me?"

"Now Ty, aren't you the one who said we shouldn't get ahead of ourselves? Now you want us to move in together?"

Ty laughed. "No, my dad's off to settle on selling the bar tomorrow, which is when I'd like to see house listings. They happen all to be in your high school's school district. And, I've got two questions to ask. First, would you like go to homecoming with me? Second, would you drive us on the house tour?"

Casey smiled. "My answer's yes, I'd be delighted on both accounts."

Made in the USA
Middletown, DE
07 August 2015